Hotel Milano

TIM PARKS

Hotel Milano

Harvill
Secker

1 3 5 7 9 10 8 6 4 2

Harvill Secker, an imprint of Vintage, is part of the Penguin
Random House group of companies whose addresses can be
found at global.penguinrandomhouse.com

Penguin
Random House
UK

First published by Harvill Secker in 2023

penguin.co.uk/vintage

Typeset in 11.4/16.25pt Palatino LT Pro by Jouve (UK),
Milton Keynes
Printed and bound in Great Britain by Clays Ltd, Elcograf S.p.A.

The authorised representative in the EEA is
Penguin Random House Ireland, Morrison Chambers,
32 Nassau Street, Dublin D02 YH68

A CIP catalogue record for this book is available
from the British Library

HB ISBN 9781787303409
TPB ISBN 9781787303416

Penguin Random House is committed to a sustainable future
for our business, our readers and our planet. This book is
made from Forest Stewardship Council® certified paper.

Blessed is he that waiteth . . .

Daniel 12:12

PART ONE

I

On Friday 6 March 2020, I received, quite unexpectedly, towards midnight, a phone call inviting me to attend Dan Sandow's funeral. It was to be held in Milan, Italy, the following afternoon. The body had just departed on a flight from JFK.

Perhaps 'inviting' gives the wrong impression. It was more of a plea.

I hope I'm not calling too late, Mr Marriot.

I hadn't caught the man's name, but guessed he was a junior editor, one of the many junior editors, on the revered magazine Dan had run for so long. So my old friend and rival has died in the saddle, I thought.

These arrangements came as a surprise to all of us, the voice was saying in an apologetic tone. He wanted to be buried beside his beloved Vittoria, you know.

I didn't know.

Just that, only being informed this afternoon – he'd kept us all in the dark – it won't be possible for us to get over there. From New York. So we're calling our contributors in Europe, in the hope that some may be able to make it. To represent the magazine. It seems important after all he gave us.

There were a thousand excellent reasons why I should not attend Dan Sandow's funeral. Nor am I someone who lightly acquiesces to sudden requests. Yet I told the junior editor that I would check for flights at once.

That's wonderful, the polite young man said. We're very grateful. I'll email details shortly.

Half an hour later I had booked a British Airways flight from London Gatwick to Milan Malpensa. The price was exorbitant. Would the paper be paying expenses? I wondered. I lay on my bed in a state of some excitement. It was many years since I had boarded an aeroplane and many more since I had written for Dan's revered magazine. Any magazine. Why, then, had they thought of me as one of 'our European contributors'? How many others had they called before resorting to me? A relic.

Had the polite young man perhaps said 'our *historic* European contributors'? I suddenly seemed to remember the word. It would make sense. But casting my mind back to the conversation, which had interrupted the usual midnight search for something to read in bed, the only thing I felt sure of was the young American's politeness, his respectfulness. Dan always surrounded himself with polite young men, I remembered. Respectful young women. They were part of the revered phenomenon that was Dan Sandow, the space he had occupied for so many years. There was an abyss, of course, between his experience and their ardour. His shrewdness and their piety. Did he have affairs with them? Did it matter? He had weathered MeToo without a whisper, to die, revered, in the saddle, surrounded by young acolytes eager to give him a proper send off. After all he gave us.

Certainly he had had an affair with Connie.

I lay very still. This is a modest flat. In Maida Vale. It has no pretensions. I clean it myself. From time to time. Occasionally I tell myself that if the plan really is to withdraw, completely – the word purify sometimes comes to mind – the logical thing to do would be to sell up here, cash in on London prices, and buy some remote retreat, on the Welsh borders perhaps, or in the Scottish Highlands. Even Ireland's west coast. Sometimes I browse property websites and study photos of barren shores, heather and bracken and pebbled beaches. I see myself wandering low hills, with a walking stick perhaps, stout boots, inviting woods and streams and tides to swallow me up, till my mind is no more than a rock pool mirroring the sky, waiting for the incoming wave that will carry reflection away. Yet I have never made a single enquiry about these far-flung properties. I remain attached to London. A hermit in bedlam. Not that I participate. Those days are gone. I don't hanker for polite young assistants. But I cannot bring myself to leave. My walks take me through the busiest streets. I watch people. In crowded pubs. I soak up their chatter, without wishing to join in. At home I do not follow the news. *Vade retro Satana.* Just once a month or so I check the stock markets. I think my money will last.

Connie, I said softly. Had I agreed to go to Dan Sandow's funeral in the hope of seeing Connie?

I got up from the bed and began to lay out clothes. Did I

5

have anything decent for a funeral? Anything clean? When was the last time I wore a suit? There was a pole for lifting down hangers from a high rail. So many jackets and shirts I'd forgotten I had. No one would care how I looked of course. Nor did I care if they did. So why was I rummaging in the upper wardrobe with my pole, looking for my black suit? It was exhausting. And how long was I going for? I had not booked a return flight. It would be a shame to go to a place like Milan and not take a look around. But surely no more than a few days. I dragged the stepladder from the bathroom and pulled down a small trolley bag from the top of the wardrobe. Coated in dust. And now there was dust drifting down onto the bed. You could see the flecks in the electric light. Dust to dust. I went to the kitchen for a cloth.

Would Connie know Dan was gone? Certainly his death would have been widely reported. End of an Era. Elder Statesman of American Intelligentsia. But would she be aware of the funeral arrangements? Surely not, if even the polite young editor had found out only today. Everyone would have been expecting New York. Unless the two had still been in touch. But even assuming she did know of his death and was informed of these arrangements, would she go to the funeral? From Berlin. Assuming she still lived in Berlin.

By the time I had packed it was almost 2 a.m. If I was to be in Gatwick two hours before the flight I would have to set the alarm for six. Was it even worth going to sleep?

I lay on the bed again, still clothed, and tried to clear

6

my thoughts. From the wall behind me came the faint keening of the television. Some melodrama was approaching its climax. I have always loathed the intrusion of other people's televisions. All the more so since I decided not to have one myself. Yet now it occurred to me that actually I was reassured by the noise of this television, late in the evening, and by the thought of the viewers gathered round the melodrama, as round a hearth. Reassured by the prospect of being irritated perhaps. The idea surprised me. Dan's funeral has woken you up, I thought. And smiled. Woken for a wake.

But if it was true that I had only said yes to the polite junior editor because I was already hoping, fearing, or anyway riveted by the prospect of a meeting with Connie, wouldn't the logical thing to do now be to write her an email asking if she was going? I could even phone.

I lay on the bed watching a spider in the corner above the wardrobe. I must have disturbed his web pulling down my bag and now he was busy repairing it, busy returning things to the state they had been in before the polite young American upset everything with the story of the corpse on a flight from JFK. You're still in time to back out, I thought, if Connie isn't going. Either way, it would surely be better to know what to expect on arrival at the funeral. Which would be where? Not in a church, I couldn't imagine. Perhaps directly at the cemetery. I reached for my phone and opened the email, but there was still no communication from the magazine. Presumably if they had my phone number after all these years they would also have my email address. Perhaps they would ask me for a contribution, a small article about the funeral. An invitation to return to the fold.

Still watching the spider – the kind we used to call daddy-long-legs – worrying up and down a thread hanging loose where my trolley bag had been, I was struck by the strangeness of the situation. Dan's body at this moment was laid out in a polished box in the hold of an aeroplane, throbbing its high way over the Atlantic. The doyen of upmarket New York journalism was heading for old Europe to be buried beside a lover who had gone before him. How romantic was that? In a man revered, yes, for his generosity, his thoroughness, his charm, his ever-engaging charisma, but never, surely, for his sentimentality. Who was this woman? Victoria something. Or Vittoria. An Italian name. Perhaps I could google Dan Sandow Vittoria. A winner's name. I imagined a beautiful young Italian, polite and respectful and triumphant too. But dead. With space beside her in the cemetery. Had the same thing happened, then, to Dan that had happened to me, with Rachel?

For a while I concentrated on the spider, up in his corner. The ceilings are very high in this dusty old Maida Vale flat. He had given up on the loose strand now and retreated to the shattered heart of his web. I suppose you can never return your world to the state it was in before it was torn apart. If I had noticed in time, I would have tried to get my bag down without doing him harm. I have no quarrel with spiders. But the phone call had plunged me into a passion. Dan was crossing the ocean for a tryst with the dead, a journey he must have decided and willed while alive. I would be crossing Europe on the off chance of a tryst with the past, undecided and uncertain. But still alive. More or less. Certainly it never occurred to me, or to Rachel, to talk about being buried together. The grave's a fine and private place, but none I think do there embrace.

Remember, I told myself, to pick a book for the journey.

II

On the Gatwick Express, a memo lit up my phone. My reading glasses were in my pocket. Saturday 7 March. Lunch. Ben. I have something important to tell you, my son had written the week before. He would be in London, he said, for a conference and invited me to meet him at a coffee house in Torrington Place. What could Ben have to tell me that was 'important' I wondered, watching the doors slide shut. That trick of creating suspense – Dad, something has happened . . . Dad, I've had an idea I need to discuss with you . . . – was a habit learned from his mother. Frank, when you're back from this trip, there's something I think you really should face up to . . . Immediately I would be anxious, guilty. In my son's case the something always boiled down to a request for money. There was subsidence under the living room. His wife had written off the car. Expensive dental work. With Connie it would be a problem with our way of life, our relationship, with me. Her job wasn't what the initial description had promised, there was too much pollution in the part of town we were living in, I was too focused on my work, my big ambitions. Connie never failed to call my ambitions big. Once the something we had to talk about turned out to be a pregnancy. How radiant she was when I told her I was delighted. Big ambitions or no. She was so relieved, she said. So proud of me. Only later did I guess what was going on with Dan.

Benny!

Dad, I'm in a rush.

I explained I'd have to cancel lunch. So if it's something urgent . . .

What?

The something you had to talk to me about.

Right. Whose funeral did you say?

Dan Sandow. You might remember him coming to dinner. When you were small.

My son hesitated. I could hear a radio in the background. It can wait, Dad, he said. Another time.

At Gatwick I was relieved to see there was no queue at Security. The place was pleasantly empty, though a surprising number of people were wearing face masks, another cheerless manifestation of contemporary faddism. My son phoned back.

Where did you say you were going?

Milan.

Dad, you do realise Milan is at the centre of the epidemic.

Ben, I don't do news. You know that.

It's coming out of the walls, Dad.

Agitated and emphatic, my son spoke to me earnestly for some minutes while I stood by the table that provides plastic bags for liquids and gels. He painted a gruesome picture.

You're seventy-six, Dad, exactly the age it strikes.

Seventy-five.

Don't go.

It was the second unexpected development in less than twenty-four hours. After years of quiet.

I'm already through Security. I'm picking up a single malt.

Turn back. Say you've changed your mind. They'll let you through.

Not with the single malt.

Oh, come on. Be serious.

You seem extremely worried about my health all of a sudden, Ben. I'm chuffed.

You're Sophie's grandfather, Dad. We want you around for as long as possible.

There was a short silence.

Just turn back. What's the sense of risking your life for a funeral? You never come to Manchester and now you're rushing off abroad for a funeral.

I'll think about it, I said and, closing the call, hurried through Security. My son has always been an alarmist. You have to tease him.

I did not buy a single malt. The truth is I associate whisky drinking with reading the news. Late at night. Or watching the news. Or listening to the news. At home, or in some foreign hotel. On a mission to collect data for a contribution. You turn on the news and at once you want to scream. Misrepresentation! Manipulation! And you pour yourself a whisky. To flavour inflammation. My contributions were always attempts to 'set the record straight', 'tell it like it is', 'call a spade a spade'. Dan appreciated that. Up to a point. Every time I read or heard or listened to an item of news, so called, I invariably felt the need to set the record straight.

There would be the odd occasion, of course, when someone was candid, those extremely rare instances when you understand at once, from a tone of voice, a turn of phrase, from the consternation in an interviewer's face, that someone has let slip an honest word. And you pour yourself another whisky to celebrate. Preferably a single malt. To flavour your fervour. Those moments were arguably more dangerous than the ordinary agendas and distortions. You poured more whisky when an honest word was said because you felt at once what a rare event it was, a frail skiff soon tumbled and swamped by the great Atlantic of cant.

I was not, I decided, going to start following the news again merely because there was an epidemic in Milan. If planes were flying to Malpensa it was presumably because the authorities thought it safe to go there. Keep your distance, my son had said. Essentially the same precaution as for avoiding colds and flu. Ben, I said, that's been my mantra for decades. Though I never did avoid them, the seasonal ailments. Summer and winter, I soak up whatever is around. Catarrh my bosom companion. I have caught an everlasting cold – one of my favourite lines in all literature – I have lost my voice most irrecoverably. Proceeding through perfumes, I was reminded I had forgotten to bring a book.

13

Of course there had been a more cheerful whisky habit in my life. Try it, I told Rachel that famous evening. Galeotto the Glenlivet, she whispered in the early hours. And every anniversary we would pour a splash of the Galeotto spirit, to celebrate. In the airport Waterstones I bypassed the new releases and bestsellers to search out the small section of classics. The new obscures the essential; that was the conclusion I came to when Rachel was dying. A sort of froth. But Gatwick's Waterstones did not have a copy of the Inferno. Not that I would have bought it. I just felt a sudden urge to look up the line . . . Galeotto the book. Like a sip of Glenlivet. For a while I studied the index of an edition of Montaigne. Of the Resemblance of Children to their Fathers. How the Soul Discharges its Emotions against False Objects, when Lacking Real Ones. I was tempted. Of Judging Someone Else's Death. We Can Savour Nothing Pure. I put Montaigne down. At random I opened a selection of Tennyson. I was eager to be out of the bookshop now. These places weigh on me. My eyes fell on the name Lancelot. But Lancelot mused a little space. He said, She has a lovely face. I headed for the cash desk.

It was concerning, I thought, grabbing a coffee, that there was still no email from the polite young man at the magazine. It would be dead of night now in New York. Where was I to go exactly on arrival in Milan? At the boarding gate I wondered whether I might be in the wrong place. There were so few people. On the plane I had a row of seats entirely to myself. How lucky was that? I read Supposed Confessions of a Second-Rate Sensitive Mind. The Dying Swan. The Lady of Shalott. For sure, the

14

young Tennyson had been a gloomy fellow. The dear lady of Shalott, it seemed to me, had had the perfect situation, weaving and singing in her remote island castle. Chanting cheerly. Until Sir Lancelot appeared in her screen. The magic mirror brought news from Camelot.

As we started our descent, and the pilot told us it was a damp but mild day in northern Italy, I felt an unexpected welling of happiness. It rose like a fluffy cloud as the plane banked over Lake Maggiore. The water gleamed. Old age has set you free, I thought. I couldn't remember having felt anything like this before. Unexplained joy. I could jet over to Camelot for a few days without fear of any curse. If they didn't tell me where to go for the funeral, I would simply spend a couple of days savouring Milan. Who cared about representing the magazine? And when I was tired I could hole up and read sumptuously gloomy poems in a comfortable hotel. Who cared if Connie was or wasn't there? I should do this more often, I thought. A little trip. A lush old poet. All in the blue unclouded weather / Thick-jewelled shone the saddle leather. You should have dismounted years ago, Dan, I thought. I was going to have a great day.

As I was stepping up to passport control, the phone rang.

Frank Marriot? Deborah Pelton here. She was the one member of the magazine staff to have made the trip. Flown the red-eye through the night. Can you meet us, she asked, at . . .

Signore . . .

The passport officer was wagging a finger.

No telephone, *Signore*! You don't read the signs!

I handed the man my passport and slipped the phone into my pocket.

The officer was indicating a notice on the glass between us. A face with a phone to an ear cancelled by a red cross.

You are impolite, he insisted, leafing through my passport now. Aren't the British a polite people?

It's the kind of bait I no longer rise to. Your contributions, Dan once observed, always cancel out someone else's. They're reprisals. Sledgehammers. The officer looked at me. A diligent young man with glasses.

This document expires on 20 March.

I tried to take this in. Faintly I could hear a voice in my pocket. I explained that I had come at short notice for a funeral and would be returning very soon. The officer again turned the pages of the passport, before finding a pale smile and handing it back.

Now there was a voice message on my phone. Mr Marriot, we are meeting at the funeral parlour Sacro Cuore located at via Martiri Oscuri 28. The voice repeated the name and address more slowly. A room is reserved for us after 1 p.m. There will be a ceremony at the cemetery at four thirty. Perhaps you could prepare a few brief words to say.

I was disturbed to find the airport cafes closed. How was I going to eat? Train, town, hotel, taxi, I decided. In that order. It was already midday.

The woman at the ticket office wore a surgical mask and rubber gloves. There were urgent announcements. Perhaps I would have to review my plans, I thought, for after the funeral. I would hear what the others had to say. My fellow mourners, so to speak. I now felt quite certain Connie would not be here. How could I have supposed she would be? Meantime I had those brief words to prepare.

On the train I hunted down a pen in my bag and for want of anything better wrote on the flyleaf of the Tennyson. Very soon I was wondering if perhaps I could refuse. To speak. Had they asked everyone? The young man opposite me sneezed. There was no question of keeping one's distance here; the seats were so close. On the other hand, it seemed impolite to get up and move.

Dan, I wrote. Dan Sandow. I underlined the name. To get my bearings. It was ages since I had jotted so much as a note. Still, only brief words were required. Of praise. That was understood. Suddenly I was struck by the thought that Dan and I had once been close. We really had. And that Dan would have known better than anyone that I was the last person to ask to give a few brief words of praise. Your contributions are all too long, Frank. And frankly, he laughed, too Frank.

I forced my pen to write. Met at postgrad. First days in the States. What else? I cast about for some interesting detail. Outside, a scatter of low buildings flung by in silhouette against the bright sky. You were close, I thought, but have no desire to remember. Double cheeseburgers at a diner on Mass Ave. It was more pleasant to stare at the trees. The man sneezed again, into a tissue this time. He glanced up apologetically. I had arrived at Harvard, an outsider, green, respectful, eager to understand. Dan was well in. Into everything. Fraternities, debating, theatricals.

Even his studies. He would be my guide. I was glad to be at his service. Not the kind of stuff for a few words at a funeral.

The train stopped. Busto Arsizio. You see a name like that and half wonder what it means, or if it means. Then let it be. Enjoy its foreignness. There is rarely any reason for not letting things be. Perhaps I could simply say that Dan was a great *director*. He directed the orchestra of New York intellect, American journalism, international punditry. Better say wisdom. Nothing would remain foreign, if Dan had his way. No meaning left unexplained. Nothing let be. I stopped. Ease off while it's still complimentary. Dan believed every voice could be brought into the chorus, under his baton, through his famously hands-on editing. Better say thorough. Again I was looking out of the window. None of this remotely interested me. Just say Dan Sandow was a great man who founded and published a wonderful magazine that brought together so many fine thinkers from all over the world. And personally, to me, a close friend. A generous and thoughtful friend. Even after he had an affair with my wife. That was what drove Connie mad in the end, that Dan and I were able to stay friends, perhaps become better friends, despite their affair. It was that destroyed our marriage. You should kill him! Connie shouting from the top of the stairs, tossing Ben's toys at me. You're such a loser!

I turned the pages of Tennyson. The Passing of Arthur. The man opposite couldn't leave his nose alone. He was all nose. Fidgeting with tissues. His nostrils were red. Reading, I realised I had read these lines before. Sir Bedivere.

Yet I had no memory of tackling Tennyson. I knew nothing of him. Only that he wrote the Light Brigade. Cannon to the right of them. Cannon to the left of them. The fact that he had written the Light Brigade disqualified him perhaps. It was hard to care about British army heroics. But I had read these lines about Sir Bedivere. Life has been so long you no longer know who you are. So many places to revisit that cannot be connected on any map. Told, I read, when the man was no more than a voice, / In the white winter of his age, to those / With whom he dwelt, new faces, other minds.

Your ticket, please, *Signore*.

Again a mask and gloves. The train was running through the tenements of outspread Milan. People stacked to the sky. There wouldn't be time to read the whole poem. All whereon I leaned in wife and friend / Is traitor to my peace.

Whereon!

I turned the pages. A voice over the PA asked us to check seat and luggage rack. Make sure you have all your belongings with you. And slowly answered Arthur, from the barge: The old order changeth, yielding place to the new, / And God fulfils himself in many ways, / Lest one good custom should corrupt the world.

Signore? Per favore.

A man in orange dungarees wanted to empty the bin under the window. Overflowing with tissues. Tears were flowing down my cheeks. I felt unspeakably happy.

And booked into the Grand Hotel Milano right outside the station. Five Star Alliance. The most expensive hotel booking of my life. 370 euros, sir. If I was going to have to cut my short trip shorter, I might as well make it luxurious. And easy. In the sixth-floor room a bottle of champagne was waiting in an ice bucket under a huge screen that already knew my name. Welcome, Mr Marriot!

III

The black suit reminded me that I had bought it for Rachel's funeral. In haste. Still, I felt no danger. I had found the trousers tight back then. You will have to go through this torment with tight trousers, I had thought. Now they were just fine. For Dan Sandow's funeral. And I was fine. In the mirror my hands hardly trembled remembering how to knot a tie. Should I pop the champagne and raise a glass to Rachel? She would have approved of the Hotel Milano, the Five Star Alliance. Pleasure never comes at too high a price. Her sly grin. I opened the French windows and stood on a stone balcony. Beyond bare trees, a mild haze throbbed with traffic. The station's grand facade was magnificent in pale sunshine. On the horizon, through a shimmer of smog, the Alps. Memories of skiing. Then an ambulance was slaloming up the street. White vehicle, blue light, ear-splitting ululation. I slipped Tennyson in my raincoat and hurried to the lift.

The taxi driver seemed disappointed. Perhaps via Martiri Oscuri wasn't far enough. I sat back. The streets were enamelled with bright light. Trees and stone and tramlines. If I can go to a funeral again, I realised. If I can make a trip like this at the drop of a hat, thinking nothing of it. If I can book into a luxury hotel and smile at the sight of Veuve Clicquot on ice, it must mean I have got over Rachel at last. The driver waved away a bearded man with a bucket and sponge. A cyclist raced through red with a green delivery box on his back, vigorous, ankles thrusting in white socks. The whole city felt bright and vigorous. Perhaps you are coming out of a kind of hibernation, I thought. I remembered reading that Abraham and Moses had not begun their patriarchal careers until they were seventy-five and eighty respectively. The best is yet to be.

Ecco, the driver announced. *Onoranze funebri.*

Glass doors slid. From behind his polished desk the young man at reception said something in Italian. Then repeated in English: Please observe the red line, sir. Taped on the floor.

I had been expecting candlewax and crucifix, a smoky, *sacro cuore* gloom. But everything was smooth and polished. We're inviting customers to use the hand gel, the man nodded to a dispenser. My eye slid along fashionably curved walls with a bronze satin finish. Bright spotlights picked out an array of feathery plants. Not the scarlet gore of the rose, the creamy flesh of the lily, but gently geometric pinks and yellows. And Bach meandering in the background. On harpsichord. A faint fragrance of pine.

I'm here for Dan Sandow.

Your party is in Reception Room 3, Mr Marriot. Even the man's English was polished. Mr Sandow is in Viewing

Room D. You can find a plan of the premises by the lift. I should inform you that we will need to close the coffin – he consulted his MacBook – at 2.45.

I was faced with a decision. The plan, etched into brushed steel, showed numbered rooms along the corridor to the right, lettered rooms along the corridor to the left. Both curving round the core of stairs and lift shaft. Both tinkling with Bach. Connie was already here perhaps. In Reception Room 3. The first time you have seen her since taking up with Rachel. Mum's gutted. Ben's voice through a poor connection, across the years. You've destroyed her, Dad. I decided I would pay my respects to Dan first and, walking past viewing rooms A, B and C, it came to me that the best solution for my few-brief-words challenge would be to exhume some anecdote about Dan and the magazine and myself, something that would highlight his qualities and raise a smile, and maybe remind those present that I had once been a major contributor.

The door was ajar. The resiny fragrance stronger than ever. I stepped in, respectfully. A burly man in his forties was standing beside the coffin. The light was subdued, soft. An elegant vase stood on a pedestal, empty. Up to the mourners to fill it, perhaps. The man turned and smiled. He seemed familiar. The eyes dark and close-set.

I'm leaving now, he said.

Please, I can wait.

I've been here long enough.

I moved aside to let him go. And there, after fifteen years or so, he was. In his box. Dan. He looked shorter than I remembered him. The legs and arms unnecessarily long, the torso compact and puffed up like an insect's. A daddy-long-legs. Perhaps because I was standing at his feet, the head seemed small. The embalmed skin had been tweaked in a bland smile. Not a good likeness. Nose tiny and pointed. Cheeks too rosy. Like a marionette. And on his still-bristling silver hair, to my surprise, a prayer cap. How strange. Not once had I had any inkling that Dan was a practising Jew.

Good flight? I enquired.

He was wearing a black suit too, pale hands laid one over the other on his stomach. I was tempted to touch. He seemed entirely removed. Substituted. I couldn't think of Dan Sandow at all. I stared and struggled. Those hands had caressed Connie. No denying it. These thin lips. He was such a wisecracker. So powerful and full of fun, slamming the racquetball about. I never beat him. Here's something for you to write about, Frank. The book would arrive by courier. It would be the flavour of the day. I knew at once I was being invited to pan it. Frank will be frank. Here's someone for you to interview. Was I a professional hit man? Or just a connoisseur of the poisoned chalice? Unless he added, So-and-so and I go back a long way, you know, Frank. Or on one occasion, She's dying I'm afraid, it would be great if we could give her a good send off. I would feel more of a loser, I told Connie, if I stopped playing with him.

But I'd had enough. Corpses are so little the people we knew. Only the prayer cap was interesting. For a moment I thought I might take a photo. In case one day I wanted to write something. *Vade retro*. I hurried out. The funeral was just an excuse for a trip, perhaps. What could it mean to pay your respects to a doll?

Instead of turning left, back to reception, I went right. Past E and F and G. I wondered if the corridor, curving, might link up with the other. The letters with the numbers. A circumnavigation. There was loud laughter from Viewing Room H, the last. Which was intriguing. But now a bigger door closed the corridor with the sign SOLO AUTORIZZATI. Bach had faded and with him the pine. I felt an odd quickening. Why not? The handle turned easily but the door was heavy. There must have been a rubber surround. Inside, the smell was strong. Familiar. I took a few steps. Gone the parquet and the satiny walls. Somewhere a voice was calling. A door to my right had a panel of frosted glass. I pushed it. And stopped.

Rachel.

Signore? Desidera?

The words were politely sharp, from behind.

I am sorry. I must have misunderstood.

Now I strode rapidly back down the corridor. Past the laughter, into the Bach and the pine. There is only one death in your life, I thought. A mottled mound on a slab. I stepped right back into Viewing Room D, leaned over the coffin and made to take his hand. Dan's famously vigorous shake. Something real. It wouldn't budge. Glued, or stapled perhaps. The skin putty. Standing up, I was aware of movement behind. A woman was on the threshold. In her forties. Lopsided mouth and red eyes.

I'm leaving now, I said.

Please, don't worry, I can wait.

No, I've been here long enough.

Confused, I turned back to the foyer, around the curve of the other corridor and pushed briskly into Reception Room 3.

Two red sofas and two black armchairs were arranged around a low glass table. Four people were talking. Connie not among them. Frank Marriot, I offered my hand. Fresh from Dan's. There was a flutter of refocusing, as if I'd interrupted a family intimacy. Giles Cleverley, said the burly man who had viewed the corpse before me. His handshake was measured. May Southwood. In her comely sixties. She mentioned being the niece of a Nobel who had been a close friend of Dan's. In Lausanne. Just up the road really. She smiled. Her fingers were moist. Geoffrey Tanner, an ancient creature, cleared his throat, trembling. Charles Porchester wrote regularly, he told me, for the magazine. Fiftyish. He gave his hand firmly and took it back at once. I nodded and sat down. I would not explain myself.

They were talking politics. Britain and Europe and so on. I felt hungry. Charles Porchester had just signed off on an important article that would be in the next edition of the magazine. Seeing that real corpse has made you ravenous, I realised. He had explained, he said, why catastrophe was inevitable. Her wasted body and the open window behind. Who would run the revered magazine now? Giles Cleverley wondered. The name Cleverley was familiar. Like his eyes. He seemed smart. Do you know where I can grab a bite, I asked, before the funeral?

The four exchanged glances. I'm afraid I don't. We ate

earlier. There would be no funeral, as such. Only the cemetery. At four thirty. Let's hope the weather holds. With this
virus, May Southwood thought, it wasn't a good time to be
in Italy. The restaurants were closed. Or closing. There was
some confusion. We'll be driving home right after the ceremony. You could ask in Reception, Giles Cleverley suggested and told the others he had an evening flight at nine.
Lady Cleverley was so poorly. Or she would have come
herself. Such a shame, May Southwood sighed. Charles
Porchester thought we must get used to being governed by
troglodytes on a planet that was melting away before our
eyes. I closed mine. Ben had been right. Why had I come?

I was getting to my feet when the door opened. Not
Connie, but the woman who had caught me trying to shake
Dan's hand. Deborah Pelton. She didn't know the others,
but knew who they were. Your coordinator, she said. I
jest. She sank onto the sofa. Forgive me, I'm whacked. Not
sleeping and now seeing Dan like this. She shook her head,
slowly, back and forth.

He looks his old self though, Geoffrey Tanner offered.
He coughed. Uncanny, Charles Porchester agreed. I almost
thought he would start bullying me to write something.

Suddenly the new arrival opened her eyes wide. You
must be Frank Marriot!

We shook hands. So good of you. At a moment's notice.
Drop of a hat.

She smiled. Dan often mentioned you.

There was a brief silence in the room and from outside the distant urgency of a siren. Again I thought Connie
might walk in any second.

He'd say, You know, Debbie, this is just the kind of assignment Frank was so good at.

I nodded and smiled.

Then everybody began to say how rapidly they'd had to react to be here in time. Charles Porchester had been doing some research, in the Vatican. The Cleverleys' family home was in Northumberland. Dear Dan was so private, May Southwood said. It's as if he didn't want anyone to come. Didn't want to disturb.

Deborah had closed her eyes again. When the others fell silent, she said, I was with him all day the last three months and he never once hinted at these arrangements. His lawyer called the office yesterday.

I got up and went to Reception. Standing behind the red line, I asked if there was anywhere I could eat.

Sir, the restaurants are closed. Due to the sanitary crisis. Takeaways, however, were open. And some bars were serving at tables outside. Turning left on via Monza, at the end of Martiri Oscuri, you will find something.

I ate a slice of pizza leaning against a wall. Via Monza was a big thoroughfare. Still, it couldn't be normal for there to be so many sirens. The kind of thing Frank was so good at . . . What a wide choice of things to think about, I thought. Places to go to feel elated or depressed. What do you expect if you chase after women half your age? Dan had growled. You should have stayed with Connie! Was that our last conversation? Through an echoey transatlantic cable. But the Italian street was so interesting. Frenetic and nonchalant. Different physiognomies transmit a different mood. Though many were hidden in masks.

I began to drift up via Monza. It seemed preferable to Reception Room 3. A woman sat beside a sign that said *Please* in four languages. I have often thought I should try sitting cross-legged on a pavement for a day or two. To understand. Of course I never have. Do not, I decided, recount any anecdotes about yourself and Dan and the magazine. There was a Sexy Shop and Bio c' Bon. A cafe called Heaven. Closed. But between a bank and a hardware emporium a small alcove hummed with machines dispensing drinks and snacks. Three young men interrupted each other impatiently, selecting their items. Or perhaps they were joking. If one were to return as a ghost, I thought, it would be good to find yourself in a country where you understood nothing. You would watch and speculate. In peace. Perhaps that was the logic of Dan's being buried in Milan.

Though the truth is ghosts always go home to fret. Never let sleeping dogs lie.

Connie is not coming, I decided. The espresso was good. I walked as far as a railway bridge that darkened the street for fifty yards or so. It must have been carrying three or four tracks. Beyond, the atmosphere was seedier. On a motorised wheelchair a man held an umbrella to the cloudy sky. Was it really necessary to go to the cemetery? And if Connie did come, what was I expecting from the meeting? A gelateria was open for takeaway. I asked for chocolate rum and *cocco*.

IV

There was a chauffered car and May Southwood had places
in hers, she said. But now three more people had come.
A French philosopher who lived in Paris said he wasn't
shaking hands because of the risk of contagion. There were
two elderly American sisters who lived in Vienna. Dan's
cousins. They were cheerful and talkative. Deborah asked
me, Do you mind squeezing in the back with Mary and
Martha? Mary apologised for her nagging cough. You'll
think I have the famous plague, but I'm always like this
after flying. She asked how the French author knew Dan.
He turned from the front seat to explain that the two of
them used to have breakfast together in a cafe in Pigalle
whenever Dan flew to Paris. To discuss whatever book I
was working on. After a moment he turned again, struggling with his seat belt. Dan was so interested in the future
of Europe, he said.

The car was driving north into the suburbs. And you,
Mr Marriot?

I was enjoying being near the American ladies. Both
bulky, both in loose trousers and heavy overcoats. Breathy
and powdery. We were at Harvard together, I said.

Postgrad. Oh, how interesting! Mary clapped her hands and coughed. Martha asked, Did you know Chet Goldstein? But you're not American, Mary said. I said I didn't and no I wasn't. London born and bred. And Elmer Hirsch? I shook my head. I can't recall. And Constance Carey?

Yes, I knew Connie.

Such a live wire, Martha sighed. I wonder what became of her.

Chet is in the Senate, of course.

I asked about their life in Vienna. Mary had married a diplomat. Long retired. An Austrian. When Martha lost her husband two years ago she came over for a holiday. From Chicago. Didn't you?

Never looked back! Martha chirped.

It's hard work caring for Moritz, Mary confided. Dementia.

Wasn't it strange – the Frenchman turned from his front seat again – to see Dan so . . . how can I say, still? Fixed. You know. In his . . . *cercueil*. What's the word?

The two sisters began to bubble about Dan's vitality, the endless hours he worked, his party spirit.

I would get emails sent at all hours, the Frenchman agreed. Phone calls at the crack of dawn.

And always back and forth across the ocean. For Vicky.

The driver took a phone call, speaking in a surprisingly loud voice.

Martha sighed. I was at that funeral too. Dan was devastated.

A big heart, the Frenchman said.

The driver spoke angrily and closed his call. I wanted

to ask the sisters how old Vittoria was. How long the two had been together. But this seemed inappropriate. Particularly in the presence of the Frenchman. At some point it would out. I still hadn't resolved what to say at the graveside. Perhaps if I just opened my Tennyson there would be the perfect verse. I pulled the book from my raincoat pocket, keeping it between the door and my body, and glanced through the index. In Memoriam sounded promising. My eye ran over a couple of verses. But who shall so forecast the years / And find in loss a gain to match? / Let love clasp grief lest both be drowned. / Let darkness keep her raven gloss. I snapped the book shut.

The Frenchman was saying that Dan was the only American he had ever met who understood anything about Europe. The only anglophone in general. The car turned into a car park. RESURRECTURIS blazoned on a plinth. A stone angel blew a trumpet over the shrouded dead. The others were huddled beside the gate. Old Geoffrey Tanner was leaning on a stick. Clouds had gathered and the air was damp. Giles Cleverley turned his back to take a call. We waited for the hearse. Deborah was speaking to a cemetery official. Man with a cap. Let darkness keep her raven gloss. Surely not. Surely, surely not. Her raven gloss was gone long before she died. Charles Porchester said, Excuse me.

Yes?

I didn't want to mention it, you know, Frank – may I? – in front of the others, but I'd just like to say, between ourselves, I was with you all the way on your, your famous, you know, years ago, article. You were seriously let down.

32

He was tall and earnest in a brushed wool overcoat. The right schools. Craggy nose, fleshy lips. Very aware of being earnest. And tall. And now generous, to me.

Infamous article, I corrected.

He chuckled. When was it exactly?

The hearse had turned into the drive. You could glimpse white lilies on the *cercueil*. We walked behind it, through the gate. It was a big place. The tyres crunched soft and slow along the driveway. The graves were packed in tight. A bristle of bright granite. Angels, obelisks, madonnas. The multitudinous dead. We turned left. Every corpse had a photo and every stone something to say. Names and dates. You're seventy-six, Ben said. Just the age it strikes. Frank Alexander Marriot, 1944–2020. Actually seventy-five, Ben. As yet. Now the hearse turned right along the perimeter wall. Dreadfully slowly. Even Geoffrey Tanner was keeping up. May Southwood had given him her arm. Mary coughed into her hand. If Vittoria's grave was beside his then her dates would be there for all to see. Rachel's ashes repose in a rose garden in Shimla. I have no plans to go back.

We were inching beside a portico now, with graves in the wall to our left, like drawers in a dresser. At the top of a stepladder, a woman turned to watch us pass, white chrysanthemums in her hand. Suddenly I felt cheerful again. I would say Dan had had the luck, the astuteness, the passion, to become a hundred per cent identified with an endeavour that was universally acclaimed as admirable and highly influential. Like a modern-day King Arthur he dispatched his jousters of the Round Table on quests to bring clarity to the world. Was that too fanciful? The hearse stopped. You were let down, Charles Porchester had said.

I had begun to think they were going to slot him into the wall. Instead a trolley appeared. The coffin was trundled along a narrow path among fresher graves. Deborah carried the wreath. The older folk seemed disheartened. Weary. But I am one of the older folk! At last a grave was open. A deep concrete pit with other coffins stacked inside. The name Bonaccorsi appeared three times in gold letters on black granite. Dan's box was lined up on the shiny edge. I prefer my graves messier and muddier, I realised. Frank? a voice said softly. Deborah was giving us each a lily to hold.

She stood beside the coffin and turned. We have twenty minutes, then they will be sealing the grave. The two workmen stood to one side, in dungarees. Had this ceremony been in New York City, she began, we would be just a few in a huge crowd. The entire city's cultural elite. But Dan has chosen to be buried beside the woman he loved. Edging round the group, I managed to read, over the coffin, Vittoria Bonaccorsi, 1934–2018. Older! By seven or eight years, I calculated. Meantime Deborah was talking about Dan's utter dedication to the magazine. A ruse, Connie routinely protested, to excuse multiple, fleeting, long-distance relationships. Instinctively, I turned to look behind. A veiled woman would appear, at the back of the cortège. The unacknowledged lover. Or more than one. Mourning discreetly. The two workers had lit cigarettes. Somewhere a phone began to ring. Deborah had tears in

V

I'll walk, I told Deborah at the gate. May Southwood was driving directly to Lausanne. With Geoffrey Tanner. It made no sense for her to go back to the city. That left two people without places. The sisters were asking for email addresses. Giles took my place beside them. He had his flight. Charles Porchester was telling the French philosopher that the Italians had lost all sense of proportion with this virus. But it's a long way, Deborah protested. We can order a cab. Google Maps said five miles. Partly across a big park. I like walking, I told her. Walking settled my thoughts. I had already reached the road – May and Geoffrey swept by, waving – when Deborah called, Do you mind? If I join you?

Unplanned, a pleasant evening began. The streets were busy in the gathering dusk. She needed to walk off her jet lag, she said. On the edge of the park a cafe was serving at tables outside. We clinked glasses of Prosecco. To Dan. To romantic burials, she said. Again her eyes shone with tears. She had served Dan fifteen years. Yes, served, she said. Not worked for. Proud to. In the early days she had thought she was in love with him. Nothing had come of it. Hated him too. She had never understood if he was a genius or just spectacularly manipulative. He was in complete denial about dying. The doctors told him months ago. He wouldn't hear.

He gave precise instructions as to what to do with his body, I objected.

She thought that was a romantic thing he had done in an orgasm of grief, when Vicky died. A sort of fantasy. Or something she'd asked for and arranged. If he'd really believed he was going to die, I think he would have changed things. She told me about Vittoria, her sprightliness, her Italianness. A grand dame. She'd been married three times before meeting Dan, two children from the first husband, one from the third. He was always excited when she flew into town. Or he flew to Europe. But they never lived together for more than a few weeks. He kept up with three or four old flames, she said. One way or another. Dan never broke up with anyone, his women or his writers. She drained her glass. You did get that Giles is very likely his son?

It was more than a mile through the park. Flat grassland with avenues of poplar. Lamp-lit now. Bicycles a constant irritation. Deborah walked at a leisurely pace, straight-backed, strolling. I tend to hurry. To hunch. We skirted a tennis court. A rectangle for bowls.

He broke up with me, I said. I was surprised to be invited to the funeral.

I had to stop now to consult Google. Deborah came close and peered into the screen. We walked a while in silence, checking the map regularly.

So why did you come?

I told her about Connie. Why not? There was a spark between them, I suppose. Since college. Our lives were tangled together in ways I never understood. Then the magazine, under Dan's direction, made a certain path possible for me. It worked fine, for many years. I suppose I owe him my career.

This was ordinary city walking now on a mild March evening. But it is always energising to be in a foreign place, with foreign street signs and foreign paraphernalia. There were spots of rain. We were both feeling tired. Deborah phoned her hotel to ask if they were serving dinner.

It was me told Nat to call you, she said. A year or so ago she had read my famous article. Everybody called it that. Dan told me to read it. He told me it was you who had broken with him. Gone your own way.

I didn't argue the point. I was enjoying her company. She spoke thoughtfully, without any attempt to impress. What had shocked her, she said, always walking at her leisurely pace, was not the idea that a certain flaunted, largely joyless conception of goodness was a way to power – any number of people had seen that – but, well, the sheer range of the examples you gave, the museums, the universities, the newspapers, the art prizes, the bureaucracy, the publishers. And the detail you went into. The naming of so many names. And the tone. That quote from Orwell's Hate Week. You seemed to be saying Western culture was finished.

When I didn't reply, she said, I felt you were washing your hands of us all.

After another silence, she added: A sort of suicide.

So you invited me to a funeral!

She chuckled. I remembered how often Dan mentioned you. I thought you might want to see him off.

At last in her hotel, over dinner, she explained that for the last nine months or so, with Dan immobilised, she had set up her desk in his apartment. Practically, she had become the interface between him and the magazine. He had never got used to email, or reading on screen. She printed out the contributions for him and transferred his edits to PDF. He went on working with the same insane rhythms he always had. The same sharp pencils. When we were in a rush to close a number I would sleep over for three or four days. We worked all the time. Like the survival of civilisation depended on it.

She shook her head. I wonder now if it wasn't simply because he didn't want to think about dying.

It was Dan's optimism. He always believed it was worth it.

I suppose. She seemed grateful.

Plates came and went. We reflected how curious it was that a hotel could serve food, where a regular restaurant couldn't. She said two of Vittoria's sons were supposed to be at the burial, then backed out at the last minute, with the excuse of the virus. But suddenly I was telling her about Rachel. Rachel was the real reason for the break between myself and Dan. The age difference. He sided with Connie. People fussed so much about it, but it seemed natural to us. I told her how we got into the habit of walking everywhere. I had owned a house then, in Highbury. Miles and miles. Not sightseeing. Just walking the city. Stopping in cinemas. Watching whatever they were showing. Rachel had got me interested in music again. Concerts. We were happy. Never apart. But when the famous article finally appeared – it took so long to find someone to publish – the criticism turned nasty. I had exploited an older man's power. She had been my employee. I was a disgrace. Nothing I said could be taken seriously. I stopped, hesitated. Meantime, she fell ill. If I had had one misgiving about the relationship it was that my old age would be a burden to her. In the end it was me played nurse.

We were drinking wine. Perhaps funerals allow us to say things we wouldn't normally. I hadn't talked about this for years. Deborah agreed. Funerals and strangers. And alcohol. She said she was at a loss to know what to do now. After Dan. She wasn't sure she wanted to continue at the magazine under a new regime. She had been so closely associated with him.

I asked her had she ever read Tennyson's Arthur and pulled the book from my coat, leafed to the page and passed it to her. She raised an eyebrow and read, And I, the last, go forth companionless, / And the days darken round me, and the years, / Among new men, strange faces, other minds.

Bit over the top, she smiled. She said, Perhaps you should apply for the job, Frank. You know? Edit the magazine. Really. You should re-engage.

You mean now I'm not hampered by an embarrassing domestic arrangement?

I mean the board might be interested in an experienced

older person holding the fort for a few years while they groom up someone younger.

A caretaker?

She frowned: Do you really think one should simply step back from it all? Period. Just because of some flak years ago.

I watched her across the table. It was good to be challenged. Let me tell you, I said, what happened with Rachel. I took a chunk of bread. Do you mind?

Not at all. She poured the remaining wine, lifted her glass to her lips.

So, when she was diagnosed, the doctors gave her a year. If that. For a month or so we despaired. We tore our hair. Then she said she wanted to travel. She wanted to enjoy what was left.

Makes sense. Deborah settled in her chair.

I told her about our journeys. We gave up our jobs. Our peregrinations we called them. Now we were walking in foreign cities. Watching films in languages we didn't know. Far from dying that year, she survived five more. I told Deborah how the long-protracted poignancy had exhausted us. Each year was to be the last, then it wasn't. We were grateful, but bewildered, drifting. I told her about the bitter arguments with her parents. They wanted her home. They felt I was to blame. I told her how Rachel had begun to spend extravagantly. There was the problem of the care she needed. Expensive drugs. Wherever we went. But also her desire to enjoy everything in the time she had. We had rented flats in Paris, Madrid, Rome. Always in the city centre. Always with a view to her dying before a six-month rental was out. She wanted to meet people, to know the world. We had sought alternative cures, in California and the Philippines. Just in case. And India. I sold my house, and then, when they died, my parents' house. My son was not pleased. Or Connie. Rachel raged against her fate. The medications gave her the energy of a teenager. She wanted to dance all night. I couldn't keep up. Then she was a zombie until the next treatment. At thirty-six she looked older than I was at sixty-five. It seemed it would go on forever. I was anxious we would run out of money. But the end came quickly. We had gone to Delhi, to an Ayurvedic clinic. She was suddenly worse. She couldn't breathe. I took her to Shimla to escape the heat. A Sikh drove us through the night. She died next day.

Lifting my glass, my hand shook. Now I have made you more depressed than before.

Deborah said not at all. I'm glad you told me. She hesitated. I see what you're saying, though. You have nothing left to give.

The waiter brought the bill. She said the magazine would cover it. I thought it would be tacky to mention the flights and the hotel. Tomorrow, she said, she was off to visit an old friend in Florence. To mull over the future. Saying goodbye, I asked, By the way, what was with Dan wearing that prayer cap? In his coffin. She had no idea, she said. I was as surprised as anyone.

Her hotel was in Corso Buenos Aires. I checked the map on my phone. It was after ten. Again I decided to walk. After so much conversation, so much wine, I needed

43

to exhaust myself, otherwise I would be awake all night, putting out fires.

Google gave the distance as a mile. Slightly less. I felt befuddled. It was cold. The traffic seemed more feverish than it had been during the day. As if the city were hosting some major event. Though surely if they had closed down the restaurants they would have cancelled any concerts and sports and the like. Waiting to cross a major road, I became aware that the five or six people gathering beside me all had suitcases. Trolley wheels rattled on the stone flags. People were hurrying. My hotel was beside the station of course. Others poured in from side streets. A crowd was swelling, drawn by a magnet that was more powerful with every block we walked. Many people had masks. But not umbrellas. It had come on to drizzle. Many were speaking on their phones. They seemed to be walking faster now. The traffic had jammed. Horns sounded. People dragged their trolleys between cars. A siren wailed. I began to worry about the chilly air on my neck.

The big plaza outside the station was teeming. A solid procession flowed towards the whiteness of the floodlit edifice with its winged horses and warriors. Impressed, I let myself be pulled along, trying to work out how I could cut across the packed, moving crowd to my hotel whose facade was visible now above trees on the other side of the square. There was a clamour of voices. Apparently I was the only person without luggage. A dog yelped. The bodies were pressing tighter. Eventually, inside the first grand hall of the station, I was able to get behind a pillar that parted the flow, like a rock in a river. A PA boomed.

44

For a moment I thought I might faint. I leaned on the stone. Yet I felt elated too and, as the dizziness passed, extremely alert, alive. If somehow I could get across to the next pillar, and the next, and one more, perhaps I could make it out of the crowd on the other side. I waited for a slight easing in the throng. Someone changed direction, calling to a friend. Now!

Behind the second pillar a boy had spread out a blanket with mobile phone covers. He made space for me and grinned. In the next rush I stumbled and went down hard on a knee before a woman pulled me up. I caught a cat's gleaming eyes in her companion's arms. Then I was out of it. Limping. The pavement in front of the great building was oddly empty. A doorman opened for me. When I asked at Reception what was going on, an older man told me he wasn't aware of anything unusual. The lobby was immersed in a wealthy hush. In my room, the ice had melted round my Veuve Clicquot. The shower was as voluptuous as any shower ever was. I had my head on the pillow before midnight.

VI

It was Sunday. I didn't get down to breakfast till ten. My night, as expected, had been troubled. One cannot meet people and talk and remember without paying the price. Without going on talking and remembering through the night. Yet the funeral itself seemed a non-event. Or I had failed to make much of it. I had come to put Dan to rest, perhaps to find some reconciliation with Connie. Instead I had resurrected Rachel. Uncanny, in retrospect, the instinct that pushed the door SOLO AUTORIZZATI.

I thought about Deborah. Why hadn't I asked her about her personal situation? There were good people in the world. I dreamed I was in a long queue, climbing steps in a lobby. Perhaps a government building. Or a temple. At the top one must pass through a tiny hoop, not much bigger than a coin. It was impossible. Yet everyone managed. Everyone said there was beauty and freedom on the other side. As we shuffled nearer, the hoop glowed gold like a crown and all around was dark.

Waking, I ran myself a bath. The bathroom boasted the same polished black granite as the Bonaccorsi monument, multiplied in bright mirrors. It must have been about 3 a.m. The knee I had fallen on in the station was swollen and stiff. I soaked for a while, reading Tennyson. I was surprised that Arthur had rebuked the knights who went after the Holy Grail. They were needed at the Round Table to protect the realm. Wrongs will not right themselves, the king complained, while you are off looking for a mystical experience.

The five-star towels were gorgeously fluffy. I slept better towards morning, but at the breakfast buffet, choosing between raspberries and strawberries, I became aware that I had also dreamed of Ben. What he had wanted to tell me, he said, was that Dan Sandow had left him a handsome inheritance and so he wouldn't need to trouble me for money ever again. The tea was excellent. I decided I would spend the day looking round Milan then fly home tomorrow. Or Tuesday. Meantime, with what I was spending here, and not having my laptop with me, I felt I might reasonably expect the concierge to book me a suitable flight. But Reception turned out to be busy, unusually so for a Sunday morning. The desks were besieged. Returning to my room my eye fell on a newspaper lying on the thick blue carpet outside my neighbour's door. It had a single word headline. *ESODO.*

I set off to walk to the centre. The morning was bright and cool. Clear skies. This has been my life for some years now. Walking. Albeit mostly in west London. I'm not keeping fit. I'm not looking for the Holy Grail. I'm not sure I would recognise a mystical experience if I had one. Or it's all mystical. Sometimes I tell myself I'm accumulating truth. I seek out crowded places and let the world appear in all its density. I clear my mind to make space for sounds and smells and all the shifting colours. Keep the phone off. Perhaps it's a duty. Or I'm remembering those walks with Rachel. At first I took notes. There was half an idea of striking back. After all these years. Some kind of testimony. The world would be surprised. Then one day I carried my papers down to the basement and dumped them in the recycling. To burn them would have been too grand. Too dangerous in a small flat. After that, whenever I found myself writing things down – We must put order into experience, was Dan's mantra – I would bin the papers right afterwards. Or if I was writing on the computer, simply not save the document. It reached the point where I would be aware, as I was writing, that the words would soon be destroyed. This provided an unexpected pleasure. I wrote more strenuously and elegantly than I ever had, safe in the knowledge that my words could have no consequence. Then the habit fell away and I stopped altogether. I was left with my long daily outings, occasional evenings at the theatre, even the opera. Occasional visits to Ben's. Avoiding politics. My granddaughter Sophie is delightful. In small doses. Life is good.

In Milan, I recalled a happy morning years ago in the crowds around the Duomo. Rachel and I had climbed a spiral stone staircase, not to go through a burning hoop, but to view the city and the mountains from the roof of the great cathedral. It must have been before her illness when we were both busy people, busy together, ever interrupting conversations to check emails, compare notes, confirm appointments. Now I set off in that direction. Perhaps I would climb to the roof again. But after a hundred yards or so I knew it was not to be. My knee was fine, or no more than stiff, for five or six paces, then when I set my foot down there would be a sharp, shooting pain. What the difference was between the steps that were painless and the step that was excruciating I could not fathom.

Few people were about, despite the good weather. Some were trundling their bags towards the station, late arrivals at yesterday's party; there was a queue outside a small supermarket, which struck me as strange. Perhaps at some point I would have to find out what was going on. When newspapers resort to one-word headlines drama is guaranteed. Meantime, Google Maps told me I was two hundred yards from the Indro Montanelli Park. I proceeded cautiously and found myself limping down a broad gravel avenue, under tall trees, beside a muddy lake. Wonderfully, a kiosk was serving coffee. I sat at a table and took a decision. Let this be your one Milan moment. Enjoy it to the full. Then book the first flight home. This evening.

The park was pleasantly alive with children and joggers. Dog owners. Soft sunshine picked out buds on winter branches. There were whiffs of tobacco, even dope. And all round me, at the cafe tables, animated conversation. I have become a great lover of parks in recent years. An atmosphere of truce presides. Time slows. People remember life need not be all struggle. I hung on long after my coffee and eventually ordered a glass of wine. An anxious father jumped to his feet to retrieve his toddler. Matilda! Two girls fed the ducks. It had been well worth coming, I thought. If only for this. And yesterday's conversation with Deborah. And Tennyson. I imagined Sir Bedivere tossing Excalibur into the duck pond, waiting for the hand to come out of the water. Clothed in white samite, mystic, wonderful. I must read that passage again.

Sir, flights to the UK are fully booked.

I spoke to the concierge from a line some distance from his desk. After a ten-minute wait.

I have just checked for another gentleman, sir. Then he explained that, as of tomorrow morning, the Region of Lombardy would be closed.

Closed in what sense?

There will be no travel in or out, sir. That is why everyone is leaving.

As he spoke, I felt a sneeze coming and turned abruptly to clamp my nose. The concierge took a small step back. Trains to France and Germany are also fully booked. A number of guests have been making enquiries.

Tomorrow? Tuesday?

The first flights were for Thursday, he said, but it remained unclear whether people would be allowed to fly.

In his late thirties, this man wore his silver buttons with pride and seemed comfortable with his role as competent servant. All the same, it was hard not to suspect a veiled pleasure in his manner as he prospected these difficulties for his wealthy guests. If I chose to prolong my stay at the hotel, he warned, I should let the booking desk know as soon as possible.

Others were queueing behind me. I moved aside and gazed around the lobby. Although the external facade of Hotel Milano had the cheerful grandeur of twenties art deco, the refurbished interior might have been any luxury hotel from Bangkok to Los Angeles. Violet, cream and lemon surfaces. Suffused lighting and shininess. Not unlike the Sacro Cuore funeral parlour. With here or there a polished column or marble balustrade, even a fountain and sculpted nymph, as if the past were still with us.

I took the lift back to the sixth floor, noticing for the first time photographs of a gym and spa bath. News of a rooftop restaurant. Beside me a woman with a fur jacket coughed and apologised. She said something in Italian. When I shook my head, she said, Perhaps soon we will have to stop to use the elevator. I smiled, but she must have seen I still hadn't understood.

A maid was in my room, smoothing out the quilt. She excused herself and made to leave. No, go ahead, I told her, don't mind me. She seemed confused. A minute, meek-looking creature. Hispanic perhaps. Or Filipino. A subservience as international as the decor. Take your time, I said and retreated into the corridor.

On a sofa opposite the lift I tried to collect my wits. Was this an adventure or a nightmare? Dan had died and the world had fallen apart. As if the survival of civilisation depended on it, Deborah had said. Their editing. I wondered if she had taken her train to Florence. Was she serious when she suggested I apply for the job? And should I simply take the concierge's word for it and accept that there were no flights? How different, the concierge's confidence from the housemaid's meekness! How perfectly in line with their roles and destinies. Their ethnicities.

Experience told me that if I went straight to the airport and hassled for long enough, out of the chaos a seat would emerge. Or if I climbed on a train and sat in the buffet bar, very likely no one would bother me until we were over the border. Switzerland was barely thirty miles away. Or I could take a bus east, to Slovenia and a plane from there.

A couple came hurrying down the corridor wheeling matching leather trolleys. The woman, in her forties, discreetly elegant. The man must have been pushing eighty. Rachel and myself, if we had had more time. Their faces were tense. The man covered his finger with a tissue to press the button on the lift console. Another alternative would be to rent a car and leave it at the airport in Zurich.

Again a sneeze was coming. The lift doors were closing. I looked right and left, and indulged. Not my normal two sneezes, but three. All explosive. Of course if I broke my rule and checked a major news site, I might understand if this was worrying. But I only yearned to get back to my room, lie on the freshly made bed and read Tennyson. During the night, amid the black reflections of the bathroom, Sir Percivale's grail story had seemed revelatory. Of what? Why had every place he looked and every person he spoke to crumbled to dust? The maid would surely have finished now. But a sudden anxious intuition had me tapping the banking app on my phone. There was the rigmarole of passwords, the need to retrieve a code from a text message. Thirty seconds to enter six digits. I hurried through three menus and found I had lost a third of my savings.

For a moment, on the white sofa opposite the lift, I

stared at the figures on the screen and tried to remember when I had last checked. My investments were in no way adventurous. Returning to my room it seemed intensely silent. A message flashed on the TV inviting Mr Marriot to consider the option of the Express Checkout.

The stock market must have collapsed. That was all. It was sobering. But the afternoon passed pleasantly on the sixth floor of the Hotel Milano. The room's extravagance was gauche, but comfortable. I took the Veuve Clicquot from the fridge, popped the cork and sipped bubbles on the balcony. Not one but three ambulances wailed by. A steady stream of people marched ant-like to the station; no one seemed to be coming out of the place.

Inside again, I sprawled in a leather armchair, but couldn't concentrate on Tennyson. Of course the amount of money an old man needs will depend on how long he has to live. You are already entering borrowed time, I thought. That said, there were people in my family who had borrowed a great deal of time. A grandmother had passed a hundred. It is not a loan anyone can ask you to repay. And what exactly would happen if I ran out of money? It occurred to me how futile the parsimony of these recent years had been when a third of what I had hoarded had vanished overnight. I could have been more generous to Ben. Or to myself. Had frugality been a form of mourning? I wondered. The truth is, Rachel once said, everyone is in my position, at death's door, just that they don't know it, while I do. We had been settling into business-class seats. Later she laughed and said, I suppose knowing it *is* my position.

I drank another glass of champagne, took a nap and towards six, phoned down to Reception and told them I would like to extend my booking for another two nights. A woman's voice asked if I was happy with the room I was in and I said absolutely.

Then I picked up the remote from a silver tray, sat on the end of the bed opposite the television and prepared myself. It had not been snobbery that led me to do without one. Many years ago now. To abandon all newspapers. Turn off the radio. I may be a snob, but that's not the point. Like the alcoholic who at last appreciates that total abstention is the only way forward, my renunciation had been a question of survival. I had realised, in the early noughties I suppose, that my profession was becoming dangerously toxic. Perhaps it had once been possible to deliver facts and even considered reflections without an agenda. That was no longer the case. Everything was overheated, hasty, polarised. There were no barriers to immediate reaction. Huge pressures built up in a matter of hours, to second this or that declaration or outcry or hashtag. Or to oppose it. And hours later to apologise for not having seconded it. Or for having seconded it half-heartedly. Or for not having opposed it. My instinct was always to question, to resist. I thought I was resisting. Newspaper editors invited me to express views they might have liked to express themselves. Or to shoot down. Views they knew would rouse mayhem. The media thrives on what it denounces. You are part of the system, Rachel observed. A red rag to the bully. Where in the past Connie would spur me on – You're not bold enough, Frank! – Rachel yearned to cool me down.

Where would this lead? she asked. Do you want to be lynched? I made an effort to fight my instinct for polemic. There must be ways to state what I thought coolly. But the cry was always: Whoever is not for us is against us. Coolness was insult piled on injury. One must live in a state of outrage. Not to do so was outrageous.

To make matters worse I was no longer sure I really held the views I expressed. Or rather, I held them in so far as I read the opposite views and reacted. But did I want to read those views? To feed this struggle? The project you set yourself in the seventies, I told Dan, is no longer viable. Even your revered magazine will be swept along. Your writers will be asked to apologise. Or demand that others apologise. They will argue among themselves. Never on my watch, Dan growled. Did he refuse to publish Power of Good because he knew it would bring huge pressure on the magazine? To apologise. To distance itself. It's a bold piece, Frank, and I'm mainly in agreement, but not for us. Even withdrawal is a form of reaction, he said in our last conversation. But not something someone else can react against, Rachel observed. I couldn't understand whether she was seeking to free me from my chains, or just wanted me to herself, for the time she had left. As her illness worsened she grew volatile and whimsical. I discovered she had taken out expensive subscriptions, ordered crystals and amulets. When a man falls silent, his enemies rejoice, Dan said.

I put down the remote. Knights on quests, it occurred to me, never worried that they might not have the financial resources to see them through. I was surprised and rather pleased to note how calmly I was taking a potentially calamitous loss. It goes without saying, the agent at Hargreaves had told me, that there is a capital threshold over which enough income is generated to allow you to live without eating into your lump sum; fall below that threshold and your funds can dwindle with remarkable speed. Tomorrow I would call and ask if I needed to take action. Meantime, I decided to eat in the rooftop restaurant.

VII

It was too cold to sit outside. I had put my funeral suit on, not because I wished to appear formal, but because these were the only other clothes I had. I sat down and ordered two dishes without looking at the prices. The restaurant was all but empty and I was able to sit by a window with a view northward across the terrace to the distant mountains. Best table in the room, the waiter said.

The man hovered while I ate. The clients here were mainly older people, he said. They felt vulnerable. Sir is courageous, he added. If he wasn't from Argentina, he might have gone home himself. All the southern Italians had. Soon the hotel would be shedding staff. It was inevitable with everyone leaving.

He explained at length what was in my shellfish salad and how it had been prepared. Then again how my beef rib had been poached with fennel, yogurt and Mantuan pumpkin. Left alone at last, I checked my emails. A customer satisfaction survey from BA. An invitation to take advantage of reduced prices at West End theatres. I opened a message from Deborah Pelton. A great pleasure to meet, despite the sad occasion. Charles Porchester had asked if she could give him my email address. She hoped I had managed a safe trip home and would consider her suggestion vis-à-vis the editorship of the magazine. She had had an adventurous train journey to Florence in a carriage packed with Neapolitans who didn't have reservations but refused to give up their seats. As I closed the mail another popped up. With the name Constance Carey.

At once I felt extremely alert.

For dessert, my man from Cordoba told me, there was a pavlova with raspberries, chocolate, camomile and lime. Or a tarte tatin with buffalo milk stracciatella. I ordered the pavlova.

Frank, it will seem strange for me to be in touch again after all this time, but yesterday Ben told me you had gone to Dan Sandow's funeral, in Milan, of all places. I had no idea. Dan told me he had a fancy lady in Italy, but nothing more. His relationships were always fugitive. I suppose he felt he could only handle commitment once he was dead, which is how we'll all be soon enough in this pandemic. Still, we don't need to go looking for it, Frank. It would be typically selfish and self-destructive of you to throw your life away when your son and granddaughter still need you. I write to you on their behalf. It seems you care more for your wily old snake of a friend and his pretentious magazine than your family. Get on a plane and go home at once. Try to be a bit more reassuring towards the people who care about you. Have you made a will? You should. You know what, though, Frank? Finding I was worrying about you, even if only for a few minutes, has been a sort of sad pleasure, since I suppose it can only mean that despite your betrayal and all these years of miserable silence there is still some affection.

Hugs,
Connie

PS I presume you have heard of Ben's new needs.

I did not look at the bill, just placed my card on a starched napkin and left ten euros on the table. It would be wrong to say that money soured the last months with Rachel. I was careful to conceal my worries and she was focused on her failing body. On the other hand it's true that I sometimes found myself praying it would be over before I was destitute, while simultaneously knowing she was everything to me and I would be devastated when she was gone. It was remarkable that Connie could talk of a miserable silence. Mum says she never wants to hear from you again! She had made Ben her messenger. She won't read any emails if you write and she won't answer the phone if you call. On the other hand it would have been more remarkable had she written without criticising. In any event, my intuition had not been altogether wrong. One way or another, Dan's funeral had put us back in touch.

In my room I again picked up the remote. I flicked through the entertainment menu, which, unusually, included a list of operas recorded at La Scala. I chose Puccini's *Gianni Schicchi*; only an hour and a half, and a comedy. I needed comedy. And I hadn't seen it before, which is something when you're seventy-five. I settled down with the second half of the Veuve. The rich merchant Buoso Donati has barely expired when his numerous family are disgusted to find he has left his huge fortune to a monastery. His poor but wise friend Gianni Schicchi is called on to save the situation. Don't tell anyone he's dead, Schicchi warns them, then impersonates Donati in a dark room dictating a new will to a solicitor. He shares the minor properties around the family, but bequeaths the dead man's grand palazzo to himself. Since the family are accomplices in a crime, they are not in a position to protest.

It would be hard to exaggerate how thrilled I was, watching this opera on the big TV screen in the Five Star Alliance hotel. Propped up on a mountain of pillows. Drinking champagne. The performance was so rich. The music, the voices, the fun and the wisdom. Rinuccio, a young member of the Donati family, wants to marry Schicchi's daughter, Lauretta, but is forbidden because she is poor. The two sing charming romantic duets while the others scheme. At the end, with Lauretta's father richer than anyone, having bequeathed himself a fortune, the marriage can go ahead. This in itself justifies my deceit, Schicchi crows. Why hadn't I lived a life of benevolent treachery? I wondered. Why not write a will that would drive Connie nuts? And what a far cry it all was from poor Sir Percivale, tormented that he had set out on the wrong quest but unable to go back on his vow. I drained my glass. Veuve is what you expected to be, Rachel, and never were. I fell into a deep and cheerful sleep.

To be woken at dawn by a loud thumping.

Thump, thump, thump, thump, thump.

There was a grey glow from the window, where I hadn't drawn the curtains.

After a pause, again, thump, thump, thump, thump, thump.

I went to the bathroom. Nursing my knee. Avoiding mirrors.

The thumping seemed to come from above. Which was strange. I had assumed mine was the top floor, since the lift went no further. The rooftop restaurant was at the north of the building, a long corridor away. I drank some water, went out on the balcony and tried to look up. A stone parapet blocked any view. The chill air brought on a sneeze.

I couldn't sleep. The thumping came in bursts. Ten or a dozen rhythmic thumps. Then stop. The pauses were uneven. Ten seconds. Five minutes. So there was the noise itself, the percussion, but also the not knowing when it would come or what it was. Then the reflection that I was paying 370 euros a night to be disturbed like this. If it goes on, I must ask them to change my room. You lose a third of your savings, I thought, and at once extend your stay in a five-star hotel. I was very awake now, waiting for the thumps to come. Or not. Those are the only stars I like to sleep under, Rachel once said. I smiled. She said, Why are you always regretting things, Frank? She meant my marriage to Connie. We are who we are. You know? We do what we do.

Thump, thump, thump, thump, thump.

It was almost a relief when the noise actually came. Interrupting the wait. But infuriating. A new wait began. I pulled on trousers and sweater, my travelling clothes, and went out into the corridor. Waited. The thumping came. Fainter. It must be directly above my room. There were three or four trays beside doors, but no newspapers as yet. Moving, my knee sent the sharpest of pains. Sure enough, by the lift, an emergency-exit sign led round a corner to a grey door. A stairway. There was that passage from the lush to the utilitarian typical of these places. The door in the Sacro Cuore had also been grey. Connie must have picked up that word pandemic from the papers, I thought.

The stairs were cement. Under dim fluorescent light. Two flights. I climbed with my good leg and brought the other up after it. As with the thumping it was never clear when the pain would come. From the stairwell below came women's voices, calling to each other. African voices, it seemed. At the top was another grey door. VIETATO L'INGRESSO AI NON ADDETTI. In red. It creaked impressively. In the dark, a tiny orange glow brought my hand to a switch. There was flickering, right and left. A narrow corridor led off under a slanting ceiling, with low doors every ten paces or so. But only on the far side. Bearing signs suggesting utility functions. Which way, now, to be above my room? I went right, stopped and waited. The light went out. My knee stabbed. I reached a hand to the wall to steady myself. It was pitch-dark. Why do I do these things? Why not just phone Reception and complain?

Thump, thump, thump, thump, thump.

Three or four rooms on perhaps. I moved cautiously, sliding a hand along the wall.

Came a grating squeal and the lights flickered again.

62

Turning, I glimpsed a stooped figure. I had the impression of meeting eyes, but the door was already closing. Whoever it was had hurried off.

I was unsettled. The thumps had stopped. I was transgressing. On the other hand, I had every reason to be angry. I waited. Again the light went out. From the distance came faint sounds of activity. But no more thumps.

PART TWO

VIII

At breakfast the generosity of the buffet seemed at one with the promise of the new day, the new week. Such a choice of fresh fruit and fine breads. A magnificent display of white lilies. Pouring tea, admiring discreet waitresses, observing the other guests, I marvelled at how bountiful life could be. You will be home soon enough, I thought. Then the couple I'd seen at the lift yesterday walked in. The two with the matching trolleys. I was surprised. It had seemed so obvious that they were checking out.

The man was using a stick, which I didn't remember. With an ebony handle. He looked older, the woman younger, slim and composed in grey skirt and pale blue cardigan. He was shabbily formal. At the table, she got up to find food for them both. He tapped pills onto his plate from a small white box. I had worried so much, in our early days, about how life with Rachel must change as I aged and she reached her prime. Decrepit, I warned. Bald, libido-less. I do, she said, in an Islington registry office. Barely a month before illness struck. The man raised his head and watched across the room. His eyes softened.

The woman was returning with their tray, swaying a little as she moved through the tables. He found her beautiful.

I'll buy a stick, I decided. I got up. Right now. That should improve mobility. And book a flight for Thursday. But by the revolving door, leaving the hotel, the doorman intercepted me.

Sir needs a declaration.

I beg your pardon?

To go outside, sir, you need a declaration. You can find one at the desk.

I have my passport with me.

You need a declaration.

There was a queue. I was thrown. Voices raised. Someone questioning a bill. The staff were wearing masks. We are preparing a translation, sir, with all rules and recommendations. All I could see of this woman were her eyes. She nodded to a pile of forms. *Autodichiarazione*. You must motivate your excursion, sir. Urgent work. Medical appointment. Essential purchases.

It's essential I buy a stick.

She shook her head. Essential purchases were food, which the hotel would provide. Or medicines. Other shops are closed. She would see if the hotel had a stick they could lend me. Come back in one hour.

I'm not allowed out?

Only for urgent work or health purposes, sir.

And the first available flight to the UK was now a week away.

Many flights have been cancelled, sir.

I said I would be grateful if she could book me a place.

Anywhere in the UK. As soon as possible. I left my credit card and passport.

My room looked different. My luxury cell. The idea that I mustn't go out was unsettling. I cast my eye over the pastel surfaces. The shades on the bedside lamps were seashell twirls of crystal. The abundance of overstuffed pillows and cushions was astonishing. Guests must be reassured at every turn that they were living in opulence. There were more fluffy towels than you had skin to dry. Soaps and creams for the Queen of Sheba. Near the big window mini-bottles of Bordeaux winked on a low glass table beside two white tulips in a slim vase.

I couldn't remember studying a hotel room before. Usually, I checked in and checked out. Above the desk was a painting. After Kirchner perhaps. Male and female bodies twisted fancifully together to make a single form, the way clowns at children's parties twist together pink and green balloons. I hadn't noticed it till now. I opened the minibar, built into the desk. Brandy, cognac, port, whisky. A golden box of Godiva chocolates. Belgian since 1926.

Had I booked into this hotel, I wondered, in rivalry with Dan? Dan might have died in the revered saddle but I was alive in the lap of luxury. While I was trying to phone my adviser at Hargreaves the maid knocked and opened the door. She lowered her eyes, disappeared. Our lines are busy. Please hold on. They were playing Greensleeves. On a whim I opened the drawer of the bedside table. There was a sewing kit, a guide: Luxury Shopping in Milan, and two squat, dull books. Sacra Bibbia and Holy Bible. Still listening to Greensleeves, I flicked through Exodus, looking for the plagues. Blood frogs lice flies boils hail locusts darkness. Do I really have a duty – I fired off an imaginary email to Connie – to look after myself? Why can't I get myself killed just how and when I choose?

Mr Marriot, hello there! Malcolm Riding here. The financial adviser addressed my anxieties at once. I should be feeling pretty chuffed, sir, if I were you. Have you seen how other funds are performing? His accent was distractingly Scottish. Pull out now, Mr Marriot, and you'll just be monetising your losses. Experience showed the market always bounced back. However, some tweaking of the portfolio could be in order. Medical research stocks were not yet at their peak.

A knock came at the door. I thanked Malcolm Riding and told Housekeeping I had taken nothing from the minibar. He was a tall, blond man. Room service is available twenty-four/seven, sir. I sat in an armchair and picked up Tennyson again. Was I really trapped in this room? For how long? For a year and a day the vow was sworn. Sir Galahad sits in the chair that Merlin explicitly told everyone not to sit in. So it begins. Whoever sits there will lose himself, the wizard warned. If I lose myself, Galahad says, I find myself. He's confident. He's pure. The grail beckons. Following suit, the others are collateral damage. Each in his saddle, unable to dismount. No hope of completing the quest.

Do I have a self to lose? I wondered. From above, the thumping began again. Thump, thump, thump, thump, thump. I glanced up and saw the TV had filled with text.

Some words were in caps. AUTODICHIARAZIONE. REGOLAMENTO. I called Reception to ask if they could switch the language to English. Our lines are busy. Thump, thump, thump, thump.

Patience frayed. I jumped up and headed for the door. I had forgotten my knee. Momentarily. Five people were by the lifts, all with luggage. They waited in silence. A bright ding marked a lift's arrival. But when the doors opened only two people stepped in. The others hung back. I was caught behind, hesitating. An elderly woman sighed. A young couple were whispering in German. Now a second set of doors opened. With a second ding. The elderly woman stepped in, the couple hung back. But from the corridor behind me a man appeared at a dash to slip between the closing doors. Which clamped his trolley. As they slid open again, I rounded the Germans and joined him. The woman turned sharply to study the information about the gym and spa, face to the wall. The man shook his shaggy hair and made some kind of observation, incomprehensible and fierce. Like a line from *Gianni Schicchi*. I tried to smile. When the doors opened he rushed for the desks.

I stood in the queue. Another fifteen minutes of my day blown. But my day was already blown. All my days until a flight was found. And, in general, what was I doing with my days? What will I ever do with them? Wasn't that Deborah's point? Yet the waiting put me in a sour mood, as if I were the busiest man in the world.

Your colleague said she would find me a stick.

There was now a red ribbon strung between posts to

71

keep us away from the desk. One spoke across a sort of moat.

A walking stick, I specified.

The word parleying came to mind.

The receptionist didn't understand, a tall Germanic girl, frowning from the battlements. I repeated and mimicked a man leaning on a stick. I've hurt my knee. Marriot, 607.

She shook her head. I would have to try again when her colleague was back from lunch.

I asked for an *autodichiarazione*.

Another man leaned across, the older fellow of the first evening. I must advise you, sir, that the police have asked us to check declarations before guests leave the hotel. To restrict external urban circulation to a minimum.

I need medicine. I recalled the man's pills at breakfast.

If it's painkillers, sir, we have all categories that do not require prescription.

And cigarettes. The words came out. I hadn't smoked in years, but surely they couldn't stop people getting their cigarettes.

We have here – the younger woman joined in – the major brands. If you'd like something sent to your room.

I felt my wrists and fingers tensing.

But we can't smoke in the building.

There is a Cigar Lounge, sir, on the fourth floor.

Others were queuing behind me.

With respect – I tried to speak slowly and firmly – there are medicines I need that I would rather not disclose to you.

The two hesitated. Perhaps the word disclose was new to them.

Please give me the form to fill in. I will answer to the police for my actions.

Of course, sir.

The man reached under the desk and produced first one photocopy, then another. We both had to lean forward.

If I could borrow something to write with?

A silvery ballpoint came across the moat. With the castle logo.

If you need help we are at your disposition, sir.

I was turning away and a tall man with a black hat, tail-coat and thick beard was already stepping into the firing line, when the young woman called, Sir!

I turned.

We have been advised to warn guests who have more than sixty years that they are at risk.

More than seventy years, the man added, at high risk.

They were parting shots. I was struck by the idea of 'having' years, actually possessing them, when nothing slips through your grasp more easily.

On a low sofa I folded the papers on my knee. *Residenza, motivazione, documento.* By *data* I hesitated. I knew it was Monday, but couldn't remember whether the 8th or the 9th.

Once I was past the doorman and down the steps, I consulted Google for the nearest pharmacy and started to walk round the hotel to the north and west. In a thin drizzle. My knee stopped me. I leaned on a railing. It was odd that for all the hardships they endured none of

Arthur's knights ever had a limp or a stiff neck or lower back pain.

Milan was grey. Empty. There was no movement round the station. A police vehicle sat in the road. I limped on and stopped again. From low cloud came the clatter of a helicopter.

I crossed a maze of tramlines. The key was not to put weight on the foot. A young man wrapped in blankets dozed beneath a balcony, his begging bowl collecting rain. Then, round a corner, under plane trees, an armoured car. Two boys with automatic weapons watched me limp by. What had happened to the world? Like Rachel's diagnosis, a shake of the kaleidoscope and all is changed, utterly.

Signore?

The voice seemed to fall from the sky.

Sta bene?

My cheeks were wet. How could I not have seen a peaked cap, scarlet lines on dark trousers?

I don't speak – I fumbled for my piece of paper – Italian. I'm going to the pharmacy.

Are you all right? Between blue mask and black visor, the brown eyes were soft. Are you needing help?

Thank you, I'm fine.

After a twenty-minute wait in the drizzle I bought ibuprofen. Then, in a poky little shop, cigarettes. As if bound by the lies I had told. Perhaps the idea of the Cigar Lounge attracted me.

And cigars, please.

An Asian woman produced Winston Churchill.

I found my way back to the Indro Montanelli Park. In the empty streets the sirens came into their own. MASCHERINE TERMINATE said a sign. The park gates were locked. *Crisi sanitaria*. I found a supermarket, queued half an hour, bought bread, cheese, fruit, beer, then dragged my knee back to Hotel Milano. My humble abode.

Where – hurrah! – leaning against the wall, just inside the door of my room, was a black walking stick with a shiny crutch-shaped grip. Please return to Reception when you check out. I brandished the thing over the silken bed cover. Hardly Excalibur, but cheering. Even better, in an envelope on the desk, were my credit card, passport and a printed page with details of Alitalia flight 216 to Heathrow, Saturday 14 March, 6.40 p.m. I waved my stick again and broke my bread. I would have to book another four nights.

IX

The afternoon was a reverie. I kept cigarette and cigar box open on the two arms of the armchair as I read, spreading flavourful aromas. Not that I felt any desire to smoke. Both Rachel and I gave up after her diagnosis. So I would have her illness to thank for my improving health. I flourished as she declined. Above all, I shut down the Institute, so we could travel.

I read about the coming of Arthur. His mysterious origin and civilising mission. Guinevere's betrayal with best friend Lancelot. It was quiet in the Grand Hotel Milano. Armoured car and face masks faded. There would be no problem, I thought, whiling away a week here. What were a couple of thousand euros compared to what I had already lost? But the word Institute niggled. I peeled an orange and went to stand on the balcony. Rain sifted down. The city was dead, deceased. And Dan Sandow, I thought, in his grave. Painted corpse and prayer cap stretched out beside his beloved.

But that was never Dan Sandow! I noticed a patch of yellow in the bare branches of a tree below. Was it a balloon? Dan was forty pages of closely argued ideas arriving on your doorstep, month in month out, for decades. You opened him on your breakfast table. You spread him on your knee. You consumed him. My eyes had fastened on the balloon caught in winter branches. A child must have looked up and learned a lesson in loss.

Dan wasn't in his grave.

There had been a time when I dreamed a quest of my own. I would never have used that word. Connie spurred me on. If you feel this is happening, she said, do something about it. She was eager to relocate maybe. The Institute of Plain Speech was to be in London. I couldn't imagine it in New York. A narrative of revamping our marriage had been in the air. There was an invitation for her to curate a show at the Courtauld. Ben was leaving for college.

I never think of this period. The last years of our marriage. My brief notoriety. In the thick of London's culture wars. Though they were also the years of getting to know Rachel, working beside Rachel. Not for us the eyes that smote on the sudden.

I went back into the room and stood between the armchairs, the desk and the bed. It was fiveish. The cigarettes seemed more inviting. There was the Bible in the drawer. I could take a shower. Order tea and biscuits. Or try to answer emails on the phone. I picked up the stick and practised a few steps. What creature walks on four legs in the morning, two in the afternoon, and three in borrowed time?

I stopped in front of the painting. After Kirchner. Voluptuous, grotesque. A cheesy joke that two bodies could be one. But also a dream. It was odd how Connie and I had survived so many years of triangulation, then fallen apart when we were two. No sooner were we in London than her mother fell ill. In White Plains. Back and forth the flights began. Did she stay at Dan's? I organised the annual Festival of Plain Speech, at Alexandra Palace. Rachel was tireless.

The thumping started up. Why hadn't I mentioned it at Reception? Percussive, fitful. I imagined Dan thumping on the wood of his coffin. If I'd said my few brief words beside the grave I could have told my fellow mourners how helpful he had been in those days. Dan, I need someone to talk plainly about gender. About politics in the visual arts. About death. Invariably, a polite assistant would fax names, articles, extracts from books. Rachel followed up and made phone calls. The first annual conference was a triumph.

The thumping thumped. I was back in an armchair between Winston Churchill and Camel Lights. With Lancelot. How all that was noble and knightly in him twined and clung around that one sin. Screwing the queen. Could it be a machine of some kind? I wondered. Thumping in the attic? It was too intermittent for lovemaking. Until the wholesome flower / And poisonous grew together, each as each, / not to be plucked asunder.

Poor Lancelot. It wasn't so bad, after all, I thought, spending the afternoon like this, letting past and present play together, Tennyson and Dan Sandow and the thumping of stout lances on stout shields. People should release balloons in the air at burials. I shook my head. Where did that come from? It was time to celebrate with a glass of single malt perhaps. As on that famous evening after the second annual conference.

No. I got to my feet and grasped my stick. Slipped the cigarettes in my pocket. The long corridor was empty. Except here and there a tray with dirty plates, half-eaten lunches. People must be camping in their rooms. I took the lift down to the fourth. It was a pleasure pressing the rubber tip of the stick into the deep carpet. You could feel the pain coming and block it quick. A few doors ahead, a wonderfully tall woman appeared, all in pink, telling her phone the world had gone mad. She laughed out loud and strode ahead, languid West Coast vowels and long legs drawing me in her perfumed wake. Darling, simply insane. She leaned into the glass door of the Cigar Lounge.

It was efficiently air-conditioned. Armchairs and sofas were all leather, the floor marble. Nevertheless a solemn tang flavoured the air. The woman shook a head of freshly washed honey. Thousands, she confided. Body count updated on the hour. A cigarette waggled in her mouth as she spoke, holding the door for me and at the same time keeping the flame from her lighter steady in the up-and-down chatter of the tip. I was thrilled. She breathed a grateful gust. Mainly oldies, thank God!

A bearded man was set up near the window writing on his laptop. I turned to study some glass display cases full of fancy cigar boxes, rums and cognacs. The way a tourist in a shrine examines the plaques. Apparently each tobacco has its recommended liquor. Proposed by expert match-makers. Depends on the photographer, darling, Miss Pink confided. She was standing beside a handsome oak table, swaying slightly as she spoke. Seized by a sudden playfulness, I felt for my Camels. The box was guarded by an image of rotting teeth, but the firmness of a fresh tip between my lips was exciting. I turned to her, raising an eyebrow in supplication. She did not appear to notice – It really will be too bad if I've made this trip for nothing – but at the same time extended, at the end of an outstretched arm, a lighter that scratched into flame. I squinted along slender fingers to the blonde beneath a bracelet. And withdrew.

She moved to the window. I sat. Her soft pacing now behind the bearded man's sofa had something vaguely predatory about it. Unless there are things we're not being told, she said now. I turned away. It is dangerous how quickly a woman's walking meshes with a man's watching. I didn't inhale but closed my eyes and held my face in the upward drift of the smoke, let it carry off my thoughts. And it occurred to me then that the Cigar Lounge amounted to a kind of shrine. A place apart, where you could perform ancient rites. Make a burnt offering.

Are you trapped here too?

I turned. Phone call over, she had crossed coltish legs, half sitting on the window ledge. Needless to say it wasn't me she was speaking to. The bearded man was in his vigorous forties.

It wouldn't be so bad, she wailed, if there was anything to do!

He shut his laptop and offered her a cigarette that she declined. I s'ppose, he said, in a strong French accent, there are times we 'ave to be mekin' our own entertainment.

She grinned. A tickle in my throat exploded into a cough. My mouth filled with phlegm. Leave them to it, I decided.

I walked the length of the corridors, on the fourth floor, then the third, then the second and the first. Rows of silent doors. By the lift on the third floor a boy with a topknot was sitting in a wheelchair. But the hotel seemed largely empty. Just occasionally the quiet ministrations of a masked employee. From the second floor down there was the pleasure of a grand central staircase with white marble balustrades and a long slim chandelier cascading down the well. One descended in wide stone spirals around softly glowing splinters of crystal. But now my phone was ringing.

Dad?

Ben!

I was just a dozen steps above Reception, whence rose a din of sawing and drilling. I turned, pressed my stick on the stone and climbed back to the first floor.

We were hoping you'd be able to come over Sunday. It's Sophie's birthday.

Beyond a fire door, the noise subsided.

Of course. Delighted to. Tell me what to give her.

A book? He suggested *Frog and Toad Are Friends*. But please, no sweets, Dad. Or if I couldn't get that, *We Don't Eat Our Classmates*.

Too sugary?

Sorry?

Stick 'em in an email, Ben, or I'll forget.

Will do, Dad. He said he was so glad I'd made it home.

Presumably you've seen what's happening out there now? It's ghastly.

In the lobby workmen were fixing glass screens over the Reception desks. The moat was not enough. But as I looked around a sudden flourish of trumpets blared out over the drills and hammers. Then again. Wonderfully martial. In the lounge area a huge TV screen transformed into a rippling tricolour. An elderly couple got to their feet. The drilling stopped. Everyone turned in collective expectation. The doorman placed a white-gloved fist on his breast. Eyes were shining. And as male voices burst into song, subtitles rose over the billowing flag: *Fratelli d'Italia!*

I took the lift down to the basement and found the gym and spa. Closed. Behind glass doors, rows of treadmills and weight stations were consigned to a cemeterial stiffness.

X

On my balcony I experienced a wave of panic. Or was it euphoria? Everything seemed unreal. Buying cigars. Brandishing a walking stick. Weeping in the street. Dear Connie, I went to an armchair and tapped on the phone. Inevitably I've been thinking of Dan. By extension us and Dan . . .

But now the cough was back. There was something that wouldn't budge. I found a tissue and spat. The colour of health warnings. I abandoned the message. What was the point? Finishing the food I'd bought calmed me a little. There was an apple. Brown bread with sesame seeds, one of which lodged in my dental plate.

I lay down on the bed and stared at the ceiling. There were no spiders here. Thanks no doubt to an army of cleaning women lifting brushes to high ceilings. Had my home spider repaired his web? I wondered. Or hers. Do spiders have gender? Do spiders have sex? I chuckled. I was long used to the idea I would never have sex again. Somehow this made long legs and pink dresses all the more compelling. An invitation to gaze into the past; no onus to act.

It was dark in the room now. On the sixth floor of the Hotel Milano. We were two weeks off the equinox.

Headlights whitened the ceiling. For a while I lay, watching, breathing, listening, letting time pluck at my body. There were faint disturbances in the silence, a pulse in the neck and, somewhere I couldn't place, a sound of water. A lapping. Until, very clearly, a voice said, The world is changing, Frank, and you must change with it.

It was an American voice. I turned and Dan Sandow was lying beside me. In his black suit. With the fake colour on his cheeks.

Why didn't you go back to the Institute, Frank? After your girl died. Why have you wasted all these years?

I too was lying very still. So still, I seemed to be floating. We were side by side in some kind of boat.

You know why, Dan. We'd closed the Institute down.

You could have started it up again.

No one wants plain speech, Dan. People hold the wrong opinions.

Connie would have helped.

I didn't know what to say. Who was Connie to me, after Rachel? I thought Connie might be helping you, I sniped.

He laughed. You know I always put work before women, Frank.

We fell silent. The current seemed to be moving faster. The night was chill.

What's with the prayer cap? I asked.

Prayer cap?

You're wearing a prayer cap, Dan. You never used to.

I did as a boy.

I moved my arm across the gap between us and touched his hand.

You're dead, Dan.

You think I don't know? He laughed out loud. What's your excuse? Suddenly he was yelling. Who do you think you are, Frank Marriot? Imagining you could drop out of life. Who the fuck do you think you are?

He was shouting so loudly his body began to rock. The barge thumped against a rock. Maybe a wharf. I woke up.

Thump, thump, thump.

It was dark. I had no idea how long I had slept. Still dressed, I pulled on my shoes and grabbed my stick. No one was about. The stairs were silent. Cement and fluorescence. I climbed in a grim rage, pushed through the fire door at the top, hit the light and turned along the corridor. This time the thumping was loud and clear. A riff of thumps. Behind the second-to-last door. Metal, painted brown. No handle. Just a keyhole. I pushed hard. It swung wide. I was face-to-face with a child.

To tell the truth I wasn't altogether sure what I was seeing. The light was poor, the space muddled with boxes, bags. There was a strong smell. Ripe and dank. The boy had been running straight towards me. He stopped dead and the thumping with him. Bare feet on bare planks. I opened my mouth. The child turned and called. I didn't understand. You're making a noise, I said. The corridor light went out. It was pitch-black. An adult voice answered, from the floor, soft and plaintive.

Back in my room I was wide awake. The thumping had stopped but there was no question of sleep. Or reading. I opened the taps for a bath and undressed. I put my underpants in the sink, squeezed a few drops of shower gel on them and left them to soak. My toenails needed clipping. Easing into the hot water, I was reminded of an old feeling. You have a piece to write. To deadline. Through the night perhaps. And before starting you take a bath. Shut your eyes. Revel in the bubbly warmth. Rest your mind. Then go to your desk lucid and refreshed.

I topped up the hot water and lay still. Like a baby in his waters. It had always astonished me that Rachel did not want a child. When the water cooled, I sat up slowly. Even so my head swam. I checked the position of the alarm cord and waited.

In the room above me, an attic, was a young boy. And a man, possibly ill.

I towelled slowly, sitting on the edge of the tub. Then rinsed out my underwear and hung it on the showerhead. I should call Reception at once. Instead I put on my reading glasses, sat at the desk in a fluffy bathrobe, opened a folder with embossed letter paper, picked up a superior ballpoint and wrote: Who are these people?

Fugitives?

The expression illegal aliens came to mind. I wrote it down. This was a luxury hotel. These people were camped in squalid conditions, just yards from a man paying 370 euros a night. A man whose sleep they had disturbed. Were there toilet facilities in the attic? It seemed unlikely. I made a note. Did that explain the smell? A chamber pot or some such. Was there heating? The boy had been wearing a T-shirt. Or a sweater. I couldn't recall. Was he running up and down to keep warm? Or because he had no other opportunity for movement? I had not heard the thumping my first day in the hotel.

It would take two minutes to call Reception, report this anomaly and guarantee myself a thump-free night.

You do not give to beggars on the street, I thought. That was a long-standing rule. I will make donations to charities. On occasion handsome. But a beggar on the street is possibly sham, manipulative. Connie gave to beggars. But never substantially to charity. Connie liked the performance of giving. At a street corner. Placing a dollar bill in a hat.

On the other hand one would never report a beggar to the police. And these people were not begging. Then, I thought, we have all been beggars at some point in our lives, haven't we? How many times had we begged doctors to give us a moment's attention? Or the man who authorised Rachel's cremation.

The thumping had stopped. I checked the time. Quarter to midnight.

Suppose then that they moved into the attic Sunday, the day after the exodus. I wrote the word down. The day after it was announced that the city of Milan was to be closed.

I doodled around the words I had written, linking the tips of the up and down strokes with loops and squiggles.

What was the relation between this situation and the much-cited sanitary crisis?

Was it my duty to report a possibly sick person, who might be contagious? Hence potentially dangerous to an elderly man like myself, and many other hotel guests. The rich are so often the wrong side of threescore and ten.

But what had given me the idea he was ill? I hadn't heard any coughing. What had given me the idea it was a he rather than a she?

The boy hadn't looked ill.

Why had I withdrawn so suddenly?

Because of the smell? The darkness?

My own room smelt faintly of bubble bath. I opened the pack of Winston Churchill and placed a cigar beside the headed paper to give a tang to my reflections.

Was there a smoke alarm in the attic? Were its occupants trying to cook perhaps? With a gas stove? How dangerous would that be? Then the obvious occurred – and again I was reminded of my night-time labours years ago, how a rambling, unfocused article would suddenly crystallise in the simplest of statements – they are in the attic because they have nowhere else to go.

In bed I couldn't sleep. As soon as I lay down, my sinuses filled with catarrh. I sat up and tried to read another Arthurian idyll. A baby girl is found in an eagle's nest wearing only a necklace of rubies. Placed in Guinevere's care, she dies. Arthur announces a tournament with the rubies as a prize. The Tournament of Dead Innocence. Quite a name. But now a battered fugitive arrives in Camelot to appeal for help. His nose broken, one eye out and one hand off. He bears a message from his tormentors: the days of the Round Table are numbered; behind a show of virtue its knights are all corrupt, decadent, enfeebled. Bold Arthur sets out to fight these villains, putting the tournament in Lancelot's hands. At the same time he's perfectly aware his closest companion is betraying him with the queen.

I shut the book. Would I dream of Dan again? Our metropolitan shenanigans never took on such consequence. Was Arthur really bold, setting out to impose justice, or did he just lack the balls to have it out with his wife and her lover? Presumably the two in the attic knew of no good knight they could appeal to. And another thought occurred: someone in the hotel was helping them. Feeding them. Emptying their chamber pot. Someone with the liberty to move around at will. A staff member. Spreading their diseases.

Stretched out in the dark, I wondered at the viciousness of this last thought. Body counts on the hour, the blonde girl said. Oldies.

I closed my eyes and prepared for the long bumpy journey through the small hours: snatches of sleep and vivid dreams, then edgy wakefulness pondering those dreams. Bouts of coughing. I really ought to have replied to Connie. After all these years. And to Deborah. More dreams. The night passed. I enjoyed it in a way. No effort was required. At some point I thought I heard thumping. But perhaps that too was a dream.

XI

Towards nine, opening my door to go down to breakfast, a woman was standing in the corridor. She wore a black headscarf and surgical mask. I nodded good morning and turned for the lifts.

Sir? She spoke when I was some yards away.

Yes?

She had the green uniform of the menial staff.

Have you spoken to Reception, sir?

I was eager for my breakfast. Of course, I said.

Her eyes, which were all I could see of her, widened.

I've extended my booking till Saturday. Is there a problem?

She seemed confused.

No, sir. Thank you, sir.

Entering the Breakfast Room I was invited to sanitise my hands. There was a gel dispenser.

We all touch the same handles, sir. And tongs and ladles. A young man gave me a photocopy with a list of instructions and advice.

The gel smelt powerfully of alcohol. I took a window seat, ordered tea and waited for the fumes to dissolve.

Meantime my photocopy warned me to think droplets and distances. Every human being is a bearer of death. Also aerosol effects. I was aware of a vocabulary no doubt imposing itself through TV and newspapers. Asymptomatic. Superspreader. At once I felt an urge to plunge into this, to learn and savour all the new jargon. At the same time a determination to steer clear, stay clean. If there were a gel to sanitise the mind . . .

With a capacity of two hundred and more, the Breakfast Room was entertaining no more than twenty guests. Rather than sit together, five or six Asian men were calling to each other from separate tables. A young woman held a croissant with rubber gloves. At the first sign of symptoms, stay in your room and inform Reception.

I saw my odd couple coming in, wearing pointed white masks that turned their faces to muzzles. At once I realised I had been looking forward to seeing the woman's sly mouth. His fondness for her. As yesterday, they chose a table and he tapped his pills onto his plate. I waited, then got to my feet a split second before she did. Leaving my stick at the table.

The buffet was less attractive this morning. There were no lilies. Gone the regimental richness of line upon line of cakes and pastries, in their smart icings and chocolate epaulettes. Today it was rather like a bakery towards closing time.

Do not touch any product you do not actually take.

Do not adjust the toaster.

Do not crowd.

The selection of juices had shrunk to three.

No, after you, I said. I had timed it perfectly. She lifted a jug of pineapple and began to pour. But do you mind if I ask where you found your mask?

I kept my distance as I spoke. She put down the pineapple and poured orange in a second glass. She was wearing a dark blue bracelet.

I tried three or four pharmacies yesterday but they had all run out.

Now she turned and shook her head. My English is not so good. I am sorry.

Your mask. I touched my face. Where did you buy it?

Fine wrinkles creased the corners of her eyes. Ah. She frowned. It is . . . complicated. She half turned to nod across the room. He speaks English. Ask to him.

Thank you.

At one of the alcove tables against the wall a little girl had begun to cough. Her parents shushed her. It was a loud, chesty cough. Heads turned. Lifting a slice of carrot cake onto my plate, I was aware that my fingers on the tongs had just touched my nose. If I fell ill, would I be able to leave Saturday? Would I miss Sophie's birthday? Perhaps if I bought the books Ben had suggested online they would be in Maida Vale when I returned late evening. Or should I have them delivered directly to Manchester?

But back at my table, opening the flap of my phone, it was the banking app my fingers went to. I tapped in the passwords. An egg timer pulsed. My couple took off their masks. And he had a moustache. I hadn't noticed. Rather dapper. She was chewing pensively. The screen filled with figures. My investments had fallen a further 7 per cent.

Dear Deborah, I tapped. I'm not good at writing on the phone. Glad all is well in Florence. Of course you can give my address to Charles. Alas I am stuck in Milan. Meantime I have been thinking about Dan. What a . . .

The woman got to her feet again, put on her mask again, headed back to the buffet. The way she moved, it was clear she was thinking of something else. She almost ran into the boy on the wheelchair, pushed across her path by a man in white uniform and turban. I grasped my stick and went to their table. Her companion hurried to put on his mask.

I'm sorry to disturb. I just couldn't help noticing that you had found yourselves proper masks. Could you tell me where you got them? The pharmacies are sold out.

He relaxed. How do you do? He seemed pleased to be invited to speak in English. Actually, we got them from a clinic. A hospital.

Ah.

I am coming in Milan for medical exams. Hopefully an operation. Now it is all . . . he searched for the word . . . delayed. He made a gesture of resignation. But they gave us these masks. It is important not to be infected. At our age.

The woman returned with bowls of fruit. They spoke in Italian. We are from Catania, he said. Sicily.

I'm trapped here too, I told them. Frank Marriot. Just a few days I hope. It is good to meet you.

He nodded and pulled a wallet from his pocket, then a card from the wallet. Alberto Rizzo.

Leaving the Breakfast Room, I glimpsed the woman

with the headscarf who had spoken to me outside my room. She was standing in the well of a fire door. As I appeared, she pushed back through the door.

Waiting for the lift, I finished the email to Deborah . . . What an extraordinary man he was. And what a hard act to follow for his successor. I will think over what you said. Do keep in touch.

The day stretched ahead. I tried the Bible. Book of Daniel. His namesake. Another parade of dreams and visions. It was curious how some were entirely familiar – the writing on the wall, the feet of clay – others unheard of: monstrous goats and rams with multiple horns. Fortunately the archangel Gabriel was on hand to interpret. *From the time of the abomination that maketh desolate, there shall be a thousand two hundred and ninety days. Blessed is he that waiteth.*

You only have to make it to Saturday, I thought.

And if I did die today? Of this abomination? If I suddenly coughed myself to death, right now, in the Grand Hotel Milano? Would it be such a disaster? Wasn't my life to all intents and purposes over?

You are at their disposal.

For some reason I said these words out loud. It was an odd thought. From nowhere. I went out on the balcony and looked over the parapet to check on my balloon. At whose disposal? Ben's? The archangel Gabriel's? Outside the air was still and damp. The balloon was a flower out of season, bright yellow, trapped in winter twigs. If my arms had been fifty feet long I could have reached down and freed it.

Alberto Rizzo, I read his business card. Architetto. Soluzioni Creative Srl.

She hadn't offered her name; she was worried about her man.

I pulled on my raincoat, went downstairs, waved yesterday's *autodichiarazione* at the doorman and told him I had ordered a drug at the pharmacy. When he hesitated, I added, For my heart.

What facility in lying! It cheered me up. My heart, I repeated, and set off north, alongside the station, under the railway lines, swinging my stick and stabbing it on the pavement. The streets were mostly empty. Silent canyons. No beggars even; there was no one to beg from. At a corner a policeman was talking to a tall man in high heels with a white poodle in tow. A woman with blue hair leaned out from a balcony, cleaning her teeth.

Now a motorbike roared by. I was swept by an intense yearning. Rachel. A great gust of physical longing. I stopped, standing over an iron grid, seeping stale air from beneath. Shimla might have been yesterday.

The smell in the attic had been familiar, I thought.

I found a taxi by a metro station and showed the driver my phone map. Inside, he had partitioned front from back with a sheet of Plexiglas. We drove in silence. When he finally pulled in, I asked him to wait. But the gates were closed. *Crisi sanitaria.* I looked through the bars. Even the dead were locked in. The grand old family tombs. The Christs and madonnas. I imagined him in his coffin, bedding in for the long haul, the dark flight down oblivion. Bon voyage, Dan.

The ride cost me ninety euros. I asked the driver to leave me at the small supermarket near the hotel. A queue stretched round the corner. Red circles had appeared on the pavement to show us where to stand. Suddenly I was coughing again. There was something raw in the air. People turned away. Buy enough food to get yourself to the end, I decided. Enough tissues. Shut yourself up in your room.

We shuffled forward. A Japanese girl was wearing two masks, one red, one black. Ahead of me someone was smoking and I remembered my excitement in the cemetery at the idea of Connie arriving at the last second. Connie was turbulence itself. That's how she seduced. Come into my whirlwind. But Dan had been tied to his masthead. His magazine.

There was an argument at the door. Voices raised. Someone was being sent away. It occurred to me then that Dan had never known Connie as I had. Having never let her overwhelm him. You don't know what illness is till it overwhelms you, Rachel said. In Delhi she insisted on visiting Chandni Chowk, plunging her sick body into the turbulence of the market, as if its churning vitality might rub off on her. A man pointed a pistol at my head and squirted gel on my hands.

I bought too much. And I had reckoned without the problem of handling two heavy bags plus my stick. A girl came to my aid on the wet pavement. A teenager. Let me take a bag for you. She wore a green bubble jacket, slid her phone into tight jeans. We must all be helping each other. You are from England? I was grateful, and embarrassed.

Surely a guest of the Grand Hotel Milano could afford to have his shopping done for him. But my helper didn't seem surprised by the five-star facade. She was focused on her charity.

Come in, I invited. Let me offer you a coffee at least.

She looked at her watch. But the doorman turned her away. Only hotel guests are now allowed in the building. She was gone before I could protest.

Sir, please to go to Reception for a mask. Masks are obligatory in all places.

And lifts were only to be used for going up. As the doors closed a figure slipped in. I recognised the woman with the headscarf. But now another, older woman thrust in a leather briefcase and stood between us. How ridiculous this is, she snapped. In Home Counties English. You would think we were under nuclear attack!

Apparently we were all riding up to the sixth. Don't they know that thousands of people die every day? Death is part of the package, is it not? The woman with the headscarf had turned away, but I glimpsed her masked profile in the mirror. No doubt it will all be over soon enough, I offered. And in the meantime billions of pounds will have been blown away!

The doors opened. Madam Business strode out. I followed. We both turned right.

Slipped under the door of 607, a piece of blue paper warned me that the hotel laundry service had been suspended. Something the management regretted. To further reduce physical contact, guests were encouraged to use the same towels for at least three days. If possible to make their own beds. Rooms would be cleaned only if we hung out the sign explicitly requesting it. There was no mention of reducing prices accordingly.

I sat in front of the screen, munched a BLT, sipped a beer and studied the operas on the entertainment menu. Soon enough *Così fan tutte* was unfolding its crazy plot. For three days, I told myself, you will be entirely passive, eating, sleeping, watching opera. The two drunken officers sang of the perfection of their women. The creepy Don Alfonso came along with his disturbing wager: a thousand gold pieces they will betray you! Ten minutes and my mood had brightened considerably. It was just a question of accepting one's powerlessness; blessed is he that waiteth. And maybe enjoying a smoke from time to time. Why not? The two beauties sang *Soave sia il vento*, as their lovers supposedly sailed away. Gentle be the wind, ran the subtitle. Neither looked like Rachel. Quiet the wave. They sang with such tender yearning. May every element / benignly answer / to our desires. Amen to that!

There was a knock at the door.

I really didn't want to be disturbed. Dorabella and Fiordiligi sang on, together with Don Alfonso. It's curious how fondly the old cynic harmonises with the pretty girlfriends as they wave their happiness goodbye. The bet is on!

The knock came again. Whoever it was could hear the music.

Come in! I wiped my cheeks.

The door didn't open. Housekeeping would have a passepartout, I thought.

Soave sia il vento, they began again.

Could it be my odd couple? The thought was exciting. They had understood my desire to talk perhaps. We would make friends. I got to my feet. The pain shot through my knee. Where was the stick? I had to hop. And found the woman in the headscarf.

We were looking straight into each other's eyes. She didn't lower hers.

I come for help, sir.

I was aware of blocking her way. She wanted to come in, urgently. Disappointed, I stepped aside. She slipped past me and turned, her back to the window. I saw her rapidly taking everything in: the unmade bed, the scatter of supermarket foods. I closed the door, paused Mozart.

Sir. She was smaller than me, her body invisible in the loose uniform. I am sorry to disturb.

I was standing on one leg. Sit down. I cleared my throat.

She stayed where she was. I leaned on the arm of an armchair, looking for my stick.

I come for help, she repeated.

I felt a strong desire to be back with Don Alfonso.

You'll have to explain, I said.

I am sent away. From the hotel. I am no more working here. No – she must have seen something in my face and quickly shook her head. I am not wanting money, sir.

Please, I said, sit down. Take your time. I sat myself. And take off your mask. I find it hard to talk to someone I can't see.

She looked around, then moved over to the other armchair. She half sat, then stood again, pulling something from the pocket of her trousers. Can I? It was a phone charger.

Go ahead.

She went to the socket above the bedside table. She knew the rooms.

The mask?

For the infection, sir.

I'm not afraid.

She shook her head.

I waited. What could someone like this want of me?

She stood with one hand on the back of the armchair. I found a tissue and coughed.

So, what can I do for you?

You have gone up, she said. She tilted her head to the ceiling. Upstairs. I saw a strong young neck. And understood.

Ah. Yes.

There is my son.

I was at a loss. He was making a noise, I said. On the floor.

Yes. He is running, all the time. I am sorry.

Behind her were the big window and the white sky. A siren had begun to wail.

And so?

We were having to leave our place. Where we live. The . . . *padron* did not want us. Because of the crisis. He does not want people.

I took this in. So you brought the child to the hotel.

She nodded. Her chin twitched. I did not know then, you see, I am losing the job.

The siren swelled and raced by.

We need water, she said. And food.

I watched her, trying to think.

I am sent away, sir. Yesterday. No guests, no cleaning. If I go out of the hotel, I cannot come in.

I noticed how high-pitched the voice was. A queer, assertive lilt.

Why don't you go to the authorities?

Sorry?

You could go to . . . the social services. The police.

She said: My husband is finding a place, a room. Then we will go there. Soon.

I thought your husband was with your son, I said. Upstairs.

She had folded her arms on her chest, looking down on me in my armchair. I realised how dangerous it must feel for her to speak to me.

My husband is not there. He is outside.

Someone was there.

She shook her head. Will you give us some food? For today, tomorrow.

Someone was there, I repeated.

Father.

Ah. Is he ill?

Her eyes gleamed. He is okay.

I wondered why I should believe any of this. The mistake, Connie always said, is to let them start talking.

How old is the boy?

Five. Hakim.

That's his name?

Hakim.

There was a short silence. She shifted from one foot to another.

Take what's there, I said, if it's any help. I nodded to the bags on the bed. I can eat in the restaurant.

She turned abruptly, bent down and sorted through what I had bought, packing sandwiches, fruit and yogurt into a single bag. A bar of chocolate. Crisps.

No water?

I had only bought beer.

Perhaps in the fridge.

She went to the desk and crouched. She was right beside me now, curved back stretching her clothes. A faint female smell. The scarf was black cotton. Her quick hands found two bottles of mineral water.

XII

My stick was under the coffee table. There was no chance of returning to *Così fan tutte*. I took the cigarettes and cigars and hopped along the corridor. Resting on the white sofa opposite the lifts, it occurred to me I might have done something illegal. These people were a health hazard.

The minutes passed. Nobody came by. The air was still, tensed by a faint hum. A soft electronic shroud spread over the empty day. How much would this be costing the hotel? I wondered. How many hotels would be empty and silent? Was it just Milan? Very soon I would have to look at the news.

A mother shielding her child was a powerful combination, I thought. Going over the conversation, I remembered how she had shifted from foot to foot. She hadn't gone to the authorities because she had something to fear.

Should I climb up to the attic and talk to her? She had been lying about her father, I thought. And what a stroke of luck that I had had that food right there to give her. It hadn't cost me much.

Perhaps she kept the mask on more to protect me from

her father's illness than to protect herself. Was that it? Or was she concealing her face?

The lift doors opened and the tall young man who had passed by from Housekeeping yesterday pushed his trolley out. Oxygenated curls and an earring. He hadn't lost his job.

The woman had no contract perhaps.

Signore. He said something in Italian.

I shook my head.

You need a mask, sir. In all parts of the hotel.

I'm just going down to get one. In Reception, right?

He rattled off along the corridor. But I stayed put. The white sofa afforded a pleasant sense of limbo.

A young woman in a dark trouser suit arrived at a brisk walk and pressed for the lift. Waiting, she paced up and down, adjusting her mask and checking her phone.

I pulled out mine and tapped New York Times in the browser. But then checked my emails first.

Frank, I'm so disappointed in you.

Connie again.

I was hardly expecting a gush of love. I know what a cold fish you can be. But when an old pal writes after all these years, I did think, well, just maybe Frank Marriot from the lofty heights of his senile ego might grace the mother of his child with two words of his famous Plain Speech. Like, Hi Connie, I'm still alive, thanks for thinking of me.

In Reception I was given ten surgical masks. Paper blue. There was no queue today. The lobby was empty. The young man behind the screen was brusque and assertive.

You must put it on now, sir. At once. It seemed I was no longer a guest, not in the old way. Though still paying.

The masks were in a transparent plastic pack. I slipped one out. Studied it.

The stiff edge must be pressed around the nose, sir.

At once I felt the loss of oxygen, of exchange with the outside. I was shut up in the stale warmth of my lungs.

Rubber gloves are available on request, sir.

I asked if I could have the declaration form to fill in. I needed to go out.

Only for the most essential requirements.

Please give me the form.

The man met my eyes. Over our masks. Like knights with their visors.

I must warn you the police are fining many people.

I took the form, passed to me under the screen. Your English is very good, I told him.

I went to sit on a sofa beside the fountain. The empty lobby was reminding me of something.

Dear Connie, I wrote, I only have my phone right now. I was waiting to be at a keyboard. I have been thinking a lot about Dan. And us. Keep well.

The water splashed softly. The receptionist spoke on the phone in a low voice. The doorman had folded his arms and was staring out at the street. I noticed the same hum I had heard upstairs; it seemed to fuse with the moist fetor round lips and nose.

Then I had it. The Austrian Alps, in April. Last day of the winter season. The deserted lobby of another grand hotel. They were closing. We were the last out, waiting on a sofa for a taxi. With the same soft hum for company. Like *The Shining*, Rachel said.

The evening before I had chaired one of our travelling Plain Speech presentations. An excuse for inviting along my young assistant. A man had written a book arguing that since we do not choose our brains, the organ that determines all our actions, we should not be punished for what they make us do. He told the story of a man whose brain tumour made him a murderer. Opposing the idea, a young Irish philosopher insisted that responsibility was the greatest of human inventions. There can be no nobility without punishment, he said. All this before an audience of eighty or so skiers sipping *aperitivi*. The hotel was proud, the manager told me, of the seriousness of its events programme, meeting the demands of a highly qualified clientele.

Writer and philosopher left in a taxi for Innsbruck, still arguing. I had suggested to Rachel we stay, since the hotel was offering rooms. The place was empty. We could take a morning walk in the snow maybe. She said okay.

There had been a fresh snowfall. A late flurry before the spring. We climbed for an hour or more through pinewoods to a small pond, frozen white under sagging branches. The air was icy.

Then I said, I'm going crazy, Rachel. I feel I'll suffocate in a domestic prison or die a dissolute rake.

She chuckled, tossing pine cones onto the ice. Lit a cigarette. It was the first time I had spoken openly to her.

Walking down on a different path, we were forced to grip each other's wrists for a moment where the path was steep with frozen snow. Before letting go she gave a squeeze.

When you've escaped your prison, maybe we could discuss a more promising outcome.

On our return the hotel was locked. They hadn't told us they were closing at midday. Eventually, an elderly man let us in. Our bags were gone. We waited in the empty lobby while they were found. It had come on to drizzle. The hotel was deserted. Happiness took me by surprise.

In my armchair in the lobby of the Grand Hotel Milano I tapped for my browser. Here goes.

Markets Spiral as Globe Shudders Over Virus.

Italy Puts Whole Country on Travel Limits Like China.

I headed for the lift and the fourth floor. The Cigar Lounge was more cheerful today. Perhaps it was a question of timing. A white-coated, black-masked, rubber-gloved barman stood behind a table pouring from a selection of whiskies and brandies. Ella Fitzgerald crooned. A dozen guests were scattered around the room. Not my odd couple, though. Nor the coltish gal from the West. But nevertheless, people, life. Two groups around low tables. One elderly Dickensian figure in a green felt suit, reading a newspaper. With rings on every finger.

Glenlivet? I asked. Room 607.

It's on the house, sir. But the nearest thing he had was Laphroaig. Facing back across the room from a corner armchair I pulled out a Winston Churchill, smelt its flavoury warmth, and in a sudden move that took me back years, bit off the bitter end and spat it into my hand. Came a peal of laughter from a table to my left. Loud voices speaking German. Young men. One opened his arms and began to sing, Fra-tel-ee dee-tal-yah. More laughter. I sucked through the unlit cigar, sipped the whisky, and again pulled out my phone.

Quarantine Regulations Feed Anxiety.

Deaths Overwhelmingly Elderly.

I stood up and walked to the noisy table. Can anyone give me a light?

Arms moved to pockets. I also heard a mutter, *Hände-waschen*. A lighter was half offered and withdrawn. A book of matches appeared. Keep them, please.

The smoke was marvellously thick and white. I coughed and let it coil around lips and nostrils. *Virus Trump's Chernobyl. Fuel Industry Risks Bankruptcies.* I felt like someone who steps out of the house, poorly dressed, into a strong wind. *Harry and Meghan Exit Britain, Stage West.* Should I go on or turn back? Globe, I decided, was the most important word I had come across so far. Going home would not be the end of the story.

The peatiness of the Laphroaig mingled with the smoke. Easy Living, Ella sang. I scrolled.

North Korea Launches Multiple Projectiles.

3 Emergency Room Visits to Get a Virus Test in New York.

Alabama Lifts Ban on Yoga in Schools.

You Can't Gaslight a Virus.

Max von Sydow Dies at 90.

There didn't seem to be any need actually to open any of these articles. What more could they tell me? Again I put the phone in my pocket. Rachel and I had watched von

Sydow in *The Seventh Seal*. Tried to. Perhaps six months before the end. An arts cinema in Melbourne. She walked out. We had a rare argument. Why did I want her to think of death? she demanded. Taking me to a film like that. I'm not going to die! Okay?

The door opened and in came the tall model with her bearded French acquaintance. She in the pink of health. With a pretty slip of pink for a mask. The two stood side by side at the drinks table. There is no point in hankering after the past.

I hid in my cloud and watched them flirt. My Churchill cloud. They worked hard at it, at a table by the window, waving cigarettes, turning a phone to show a photograph. He laughed out loud. He seemed a pleasant man. She shook out her long hair, fished in a handbag. Ella's voice oozed. Glancing at a few more headlines – *Weinstein Appealed to Bloomberg, No Freedom Without Health* – I was struck by how little of my past was present to me now. The early days with Connie, Ben's childhood. Crushed to mulch with the weight of the years. Now they were taking a selfie, which allowed his hand to steady hers.

Economy Faces Tornado Headwind.

I rested my cigar on the ashtray. It was a relief to feel no emotional response to any of this. No anger at all. Nor even much curiosity. The one thing that really remains, I thought, is Rachel. The one anger her disease. Would either of these two turtledoves remember this evening in their seventies? And the one great regret our arguments at the end. You don't want me to be cured! You're evil! I drained the Laphroaig. Why, I wondered, were Ben and Connie so worried for me? When I die Ben will have my money without needing to ask. Sophie will have all she needs. A charming child. Five on Sunday. Same age as Hakim. We will have fun.

XIII

The corridors were empty and stale. I was used to fresh air. At least London air. But if this was the only way to get any exercise, so be it. A man who is tired of London is tired of life. Soon I would be home. On the other hand, what is so wrong with being tired of life? When the time comes.

I rested. Examined a row of old prints. Each corridor had its theme. Vintage cars on the fourth floor, measuring the space between one luxury room and the next. Italian monuments on the fifth. Colosseum. Tower of Pisa. On the sixth, costumes at La Scala. Don Giovanni. Rigoletto. No one looked at them. Like objects in a tomb.

Apply for Dan's job, Deborah said. Get involved again.

I had reached the rooftop restaurant. Closed. A REDUCED MENU will be served in the BREAKFAST ROOM on the FIRST FLOOR between 19.30 and 21.30. Please SANITISE YOUR HANDS.

Alternatively you could fall ill. Be rushed to hospital. Then you would really be in the thick of it.

If the lifts weren't to be used to go down, it would have to be the stairs. But stepping down onto my bad knee was painful. At the fourth I took the lift and the hell with it.

At the third it stopped. I was facing the boy on his wheel-chair. Was he in Milan for medical tests too? His minder, in white dungarees, did not push him in.

Sir, in the lifts you must go only up. A menial was on guard in the lobby. I brandished Excalibur and pushed by. The Breakfast Room was at the end of the corridor.

At my table I closed the *New York Times* and switched to the *Guardian*. *This is a Meltdown. Tension Turns to Panic. Mexican Women Protest Femicide.*

Still here, sir!

It was my Argentinian waiter of Sunday evening.

You too, I said.

We are few now. He made his eyes rueful and described the three dishes on offer.

I chose the risotto, with veal meatballs.

But the restaurant was surprisingly busy this evening. Faces were becoming familiar. The indignant business-woman. The man with the black tailcoat and his family. Presumably Hasidic Jews. The men at their separate tables. People have nowhere else to eat, I realised. Our gourmet restaurant had become a prison canteen. Checking my email, the name Porchester appeared.

Dear Frank, I wanted you to know that after much reflection and with full knowledge of the awesome responsibility it entails I have put myself forward for Dan's job. I was wondering if you might be so good as to join the select circle of those who have written a word or two to the board to endorse my candidature. You will find three recent articles of mine attached to give an idea of my position on the main issues of the day. Also the names of other supporters. I have always been a great admirer of your integrity and spirit. Certainly it would be good to see your sharp analyses in the magazine once more. Charles.

The risotto was rich and spicy. My waiter had proposed a glass of Barbera. Rolling it round my mouth, I saw my odd couple being led to a table. They were arm in arm. The old man seemed excited and talkative. But now Connie popped up. Communication is compulsive.

Frank, to prepare you for Sophie's birthday party . . . A month or so ago Patricia was involved in a car accident. Her fault. An elderly man is in a coma. There is to be a court case but Ben isn't satisfied with the legal aid lawyer and wants to go private. I shall say no more . . .

As I headed for the door, Alberto Rizzo waved. I made a small detour.

Any luck? I asked.

The hospital is very busy. We are waiting. Hoping.

Fingers crossed, I said. His partner glanced up from her food, twisted her mouth and looked down again.

In the lift I remembered I had told Rachel, right at the start, that when I went – long before her no doubt – she should not hesitate to find herself another . . . She had put a hand over my mouth. I could feel the cool skin on my lips, now, in the moist warmth behind my mask, shooting up to the sixth floor of the Hotel Milano.

It was not a good time for meeting strangers.

The room had a tired smell. Each day feels harder, I thought. Tomorrow I must sort out a better strategy. Then, stepping out of a long shower, I was aware of a noise. A buzzing, on and off. I poked my head out of the bathroom.

The noise had stopped. I towelled myself dry and hopped into the room. It began again. An intermittent buzz, with resonance. I picked up Excalibur and went out on the balcony, naked in the cold damp air. Why? Why was I deliberately doing stuff that was odd? Things that quickened the senses. I grasped the stone parapet and leaned over, the gritty surface against my thighs. The balloon was still there, caught in the branches. Company.

I went back inside and closed the big windows. The sound had stopped. For a moment it crossed my mind I was losing it. This is dementia. I pulled on my T-shirt to sleep, and as my head came out through the neck, saw her phone on the bedside table. On top of Tennyson. A green LED shone in one corner. Fully charged.

It was a surprisingly expensive-looking thing. I fiddled. The screen lit up with five people arm in arm. In a walled garden, with a tree. The women were wearing headscarves. Three notifications in Arabic script. A swipe pattern to block access.

So she would have to come back. There would be a knock at the door. Perhaps she had already tried. I would cover myself in my dressing gown and take it to her. There was no point in falling asleep before that happened.

Back to Tennyson then. Bored with Arthur, I leafed back and forth. Ulysses.

It little profits that an idle king,
By this still hearth . . .

114

The phone began to vibrate.

I watched it. Arabic appeared. A name? It rang four times, five. It was extraordinary how this riveted my attention. Eight times, nine. Should I answer?

It stopped. I examined the phone again, but there seemed to be no way to get into the settings and mute it. Back to Ithaca.

I cannot rest from travel: I will drink
Life to the lees.

Clearly, I thought, Homer's hero didn't have a bad knee. I bent back the spine of the book, wondering if I mightn't have been happier after all with Montaigne.

Much have I seen and known; cities of men
And manners, climates, councils, governments.
Myself not least, but honour'd of them all.

I wish! Who gets to be honoured worldwide these days? The answer came at once. Dan.

And drunk delight of battle with my peers . . .
Delight of battle!

I stopped. I was feeling a little nauseous. The risotto perhaps, or the cold air on the balcony. For me battle became a misery. I had been overwhelmed.

How dull it is to pause, to make an end,
To rust unburnish'd, not to shine in use!
Not at all!

The phone was ringing again. It pulsed. Again the Arabic script lit up. I waited. It rang on and on.

I put the book down and slid my finger on the screen.

A voice spoke. A deep guttural voice.

I am sorry, I cut in, I am not the owner of this phone.

There was a pause. Then more incomprehensible speech. It sounded aggressive.

The owner left the phone in my room. No doubt she will come back for it soon enough.

Again the voice.

I'm afraid I can't understand you.

The caller rang off. I put the phone down. I felt strangely shaken. I picked up Tennyson, smoothed down the page, then flung the book across the room. This was ridiculous. Should I take the phone up to the attic?

I was tired. I had already undressed.

I sat in this state for some minutes. Propped up on soft pillows. Retrieve the book? Smoke a cigarette on the balcony? Pour a drink from the minibar? Wander the corridors of the hotel? I was bursting with tension.

When the phone rang again I picked it up, weighed it in my hand, pulsing and vibrating with its foreignness, then tossed it across the room after Ulysses. It caught the leg of the coffee table and banged on the floor. Silent.

I slid down under the sheets. In the dark. In the quiet. I turned on my side. There was no thumping tonight. I could sleep.

I couldn't sleep. I turned on my back. Why had I done that?

I resisted a few minutes, then swung my legs off the bed and felt for the light switch.

The screen of the phone was cracked diagonally. Was it working? I pressed the buttons on the side. Nothing.

For a moment I stood in the middle of the room. In the T-shirt I'd brought to sleep in. What was all this about?

I dressed. My travelling clothes this time. Everything smelt stale. I took my stick and headed for the stairs.

The hotel's ubiquitous electric hum seemed more present than ever. I passed through the grey door that led from luxury to utility and climbed the cement stairs to the warning, SOLO AUTORIZZATI. Fluorescent light flickered along the corridor.

Which door was it? Second from the end? They were all alike.

I stood facing it. A low door. You almost had to bend. Old brown paint. Overlooked in the recent renovation. I pulled out the phone and pressed its buttons again. The corridor lights went out.

Pitch-dark. This time I knocked. Softly. The hum didn't reach up here. There was no response. No sound at all.

I knocked again.

Why hadn't she come back for her phone at once? This could so easily have been avoided.

I put a hand on the door and pushed. It was Tuesday evening. Wednesday, Thursday and Friday to get through.

The door squeaked. I had the impression there had been another sound too, inside. Perhaps not. I swayed a little in the dark, prodding my stick in front of me, as if in dread of a chasm. And the smell hit me. Damp, sour and thick. I held the doorpost.

Is anybody here? It's the man from downstairs.

I stood, listening. In the dark. Then tried another step, holding on to my stick.

I have brought your phone for you.

Something brushed against my ankle. I stepped sharply

back and banged against the doorpost. Stumbled. Let out a yell.

A light clicked on. A low wall of boxes appeared, dividing the near space from the far. The lamp must be on the floor beyond the boxes. A black cat meowed.

Now a head and shoulders appeared above the boxes. She must be kneeling. Without headscarf or mask. A round face in blotches of chiaroscuro. She ducked down. One moment, please.

I'm afraid I tripped on the stairs and it fell. I hope it isn't broken.

A child whined. There was whispered scolding. Beyond the boxes the roof slanted steeply down. They must be sleeping on the floor. To my right, against the wall, in the shadows, there were stacks of tiles, rolls of carpet.

Now she reappeared with a mask and headscarf, wrapped in a white bathrobe. Property of the hotel. There was a gap in the boxes to the left.

I'm afraid I slipped on the stairs.

She came to me, treading carefully in the clutter, took the phone, pressed the buttons, rubbed the screen, examined the crack. She seemed a different presence here. Swift and sure of herself.

It is broken. She looked up.

So stupid of me. It's my knee.

The little boy had followed her. In pyjamas and fleece, barefoot. He hugged her legs. She was still fiddling with the phone.

From behind the boxes a voice spoke weakly. She turned and answered. And her voice changed. It was warm and cooing. The boy peeked from behind her back and made faces. I winked at him.

Someone was trying to call you. It kept ringing. That's why I came up. I'm sorry.

From behind the boxes came a low cough.

If you want to use my phone, please do.

I pulled it from my pocket.

She hesitated, eyes alive with caution.

The boy fussed for her attention, tugging at the gown, which was too big for her, almost hiding her hands.

I don't know the numbers, she said.

Ah.

Wait. She turned and went back behind the barrier of boxes, dropped down. There were low voices. She hadn't called me sir, I realised.

The boy let out a sudden high-pitched trill. He sunk on his haunches. A queer, wheedling sound. After the cat. The animal had taken refuge behind a roll of carpet. The child made frog-like jumps in that direction. Showing off.

Hakim, I said.

He turned, pouted, turned back. Behind the boxes the confabulation went on. I sat down on a stack of tiles.

Hakim.

Again he pouted and scowled. I smiled. When he got close, the cat shot off along the wall, leaping over the boxes. The boy scrambled after it with a yell. The mother stood to shush him.

Why not just go? I thought. Back to my warm bed. I hadn't meant to break her phone. What was the point of feeling guilty? The cat reappeared, perching on the boxes, studying me. Unblinking.

It is okay, the woman said. It is my husband that called. I am sure.

She came back and squatted a yard or so away from me. Bouncing very gently as she spoke.

Perhaps he has found a flat for you.

Between her eyes, the skin wrinkled. Yes. Maybe.

Is your father ill?

She didn't reply.

Suddenly I was irritated. I got to my feet.

Look, why don't you just tell the hotel management what the situation is and ask for help? Then you can go to the place your husband has found. I can give you money for another phone.

She was squatting on her haunches, watching me.

It's not good for you to be here. It's cold. Dirty. With the boy as well. There's no bathroom.

On my feet, I meant to go to the door. Then I sat down again, on the tiles.

Nothing is more important than health, I said. You'll be looked after.

She let out a sort of growl. A strange cry. Her son came running. He put his arms round her back and his face beside hers.

I'm really sorry about the phone. It was stupid of me.

She stood up, surprising the boy who tumbled from her back.

Please go now, she said.

XIV

I went to breakfast in my coat, took more than I needed at the buffet and slipped croissants and apples into my pockets. Then found myself glancing at headlines with a certain ease. *Italians Staying Home. 600 deaths. Five Things We have Learned about Self Isolation. Allegations against Placido Domingo Deemed Credible.* Perhaps I could go out, I thought, and buy the woman a phone. It was Wednesday. My odd couple didn't show. The Frenchman appeared, on his own. To my surprise, he nodded his mask my way, as if we were acquainted. The angry businesswoman ate scrambled eggs over her laptop.

Looking across the room, its sumptuous furnishings and attentive staff, I wondered at the life of the woman in the attic. The life of the child. I wondered at the focus and practicality I had felt in her presence. Her attentiveness with her mask and headscarf. The affection in her high cooing voice. Her ease crouching down, only moments after being woken. Also her state of unsurprise. As if it were not so unusual to hide one's family plus cat in a hotel attic. Who could tell what experiences such people were coming from? What journeys they had made. Surely if the father were well, he would have come forward and spoken to me, if only to offer a protective presence for his daughter.

I thought over our encounter, her reaction to the loss of her phone, which presumably was her only contact with the world outside the hotel. Or did the father have one? But if he did, wouldn't her husband have called him? Not finding his wife on hers. Perhaps he had. Or was the battery dead? But then why not ask me to charge it? And why sit looking at me like that for so long, then ask nothing. Then send me away.

I ate a fruit salad. I had slept badly. But that was par for the course. I decided not to reply to Charles Porchester. You must be a long way from that precious keyboard . . . Connie had written. Her old love affair with suspension points. I looked up Dan's magazine. The website. *Liberalism, the Challenge*, was the lead article. Then, *Academe's Anxieties*. It was hard to imagine taking out a subscription. On Amazon, sipping tea, I found *Frog and Toad Are Friends* and *We Don't Eat Our Classmates*. It's the first day of school for Penelope Rex, and she can't wait to meet her classmates. But it's hard to make human friends when they're so darn delicious! Also a biography of Alfred Lord Tennyson. *To Strive, to Seek, to Find*. I selected one-day delivery. The Ulysses thing was beautiful nonsense, I decided. Old men embarking on wild adventures.

Back on the sixth floor, I was fumbling for my keycard when I felt a tug on my raincoat. For a split second I imagined a hotel detective stopping me for stealing food. It was Hakim. Bedraggled. He was holding a piece of

paper. With the hotel logo. And the words: FOOD AND
WATER. THANK YOU.

I caught his shoulder.

Hang on!

He was twisting, pouting.

Wait!

Hand on the pommel of my stick, I pulled a croissant
from my pocket. A buttery fragrance filled the air. He shot
out a small hand.

Let's find a bag. I went into the room. He stood at the
open door, shifting from one foot to the other, like his
mother. I fished a supermarket bag from the waste bin.

Would you like a shower?

The bathroom was just inside the room. Its door open.

Shower? I turned on the light, went in, leaned into the
shower, swivelled the lever.

Yes? Smell nice?

The water splashed. He peeped in. I held out a hand. He
seemed puzzled. His face was so mobile. Then he turned
and ran. From baldness and mottled skin, no doubt. I
watched him scampering off down the corridor, the bag
banging against his ankles.

The question now was, could I get past the doorman
again? Or rather doormen. There were two. At least you
have something to do, I thought. You're not idle. Though
the revolving doors of the Hotel Milano were hardly the
Pillars of Hercules. Walking down the stairs from the sixth,
one chary step at a time – to comply, to pass the morning – I
remembered having told myself the same thing in Rachel's

last days: at least it's clear now what you have to do, for however long it takes.

Sitting on a sofa in Reception, I watched how it worked. Everyone who passed through must have their temperature taken, and must show and justify their *autodichiarazione*. Perhaps it was encouraging for these men to have a real job at last. They had felt rusty, unburnish'd. The Indian boy was wheeled out, blankets heaped on his knees. An ambulance was waiting. The young German business people were allowed through. But the woman from the odd couple was turned back.

I watched. She must have come from the stairs behind me, across the polished marble. Suddenly she was in my line of vision, striding towards the doors, guarded by the two men in their crimson uniforms, their gloves. She was wearing dark trousers, flat shoes, a beige coat. They barred her way. Voices were raised. She spoke sharply, rapidly, impatient and tearful. She had no piece of paper. She tried to push past. The concierge hurried to intervene. She was beside herself. I couldn't understand a word. She pulled down her mask. Her colour came up. The men were implacable. Pressing their masks to their faces. Anxious perhaps. Until, at the climax, as they were trying to escort her back to the lift and she was half resisting, a trumpet blared out. The same three blasts I had heard here before. Faces turned to the big wall screen. Once again it rippled with national pride, the red white and green. As the choir burst into song, I hobbled quickly to the door and slipped out, free.

There was pale sunshine, volumes of fresh air. What

a relief. A young man was standing against a tree trunk across from the taxi rank. Smoking. Possibly Arab. Could it be the husband? Wearing bubble jacket and jeans. If she had given me his name I could have tried to speak to him. Round the corner, four policemen were blocking the pavement. It was too late to change direction. I had the first day's *autodichiarazione* in my pocket. I waited while they laughed with a young woman carrying a backpack. It all seemed friendly enough.

I am going to the pharmacy. For medicine.

They studied my *autodichiarazione*, which had a crumpled look. And no date.

Grand Hotel Milano, one muttered. The young men weighed me up.

When you have your medicine you are returning to the hotel.

At once.

You are American?

English.

Why are you coming in Italy?

For a funeral.

They spoke to each other. They seemed to be growing more hostile, as though they had smelt a rat. I looked shabby, hadn't shaved. They wore masks which they kept adjusting with gloved hands.

Which medicine?

Of who is the funeral?

I turned from one to the other. His name was Dan Sandow, I said. An American. I need cortisone. For my knee.

You have the recipe?

Sorry?

You have the paper. From the doctor.

No.

Your document, please.

They examined my passport, passing it from hand to hand. I was a curiosity. They were deciding whether to make trouble. Other pedestrians passed by, careful not to look. Some masked, some not. I had the packet of masks in my coat pocket. Watching the men as they passed the passport around, I felt a curious mix of anxiety and pleasure. Stuff was happening. I was dealing with it.

Signore, this document stops. The 20 this month.

I am returning to London on Saturday. That's the 14th, I think.

No person is entering or leaving Lombardy.

I have a flight with Alitalia. From Linate. The hotel made the booking.

They discussed this. There was something they weren't sure of. One older man and three younger. The older man pulled out a phone and took a photo of my passport and *autodichiarazione*.

We are checking this.

I was surprised by my acquiescence. Even a week ago I would have protested. Now I wasn't even seething. No thoughts of wielding Excalibur.

You understand you only go out from the hotel room for essential things.

Of course.

They all stood, looking at me. I was leaning on my stick. Hamming it.

The man holding my passport said, You are born in 1944 so you are seventy-six. He shook his head. Not good for this virus.

I'm seventy-five, I said. My birthday is in June.

They laughed and the man handed back the document. We hope you are celebrating that birthday, *Signore*.

In the queue outside the supermarket I thought of birthdays. The child loves the day when everybody pays attention. Sophie on Sunday. The self swells towards grown-upness. But at my age, why celebrate another reminder of time running out? Another nail in the coffin. Or are we to believe in fullness, plenitude? A day when others remember your longevity, achievements even.

Then I was struck by the question, do the things you do attach to you? The good and the bad? The criminal his crime. The philanthropist his gifts. Allegations against Placido Domingo Deemed Credible. Is Frank Marriot the man who wrote Power of Good, devised the Institute of Plain Speech, gave his heart to Rachel? Or the man who, in a moment of childish pique, threw a desperate woman's phone across his luxury hotel room?

The guardian on the door of the supermarket was speaking to me.

I shook my head.

He spoke some more. A burly man, mask tight on fat cheeks. Wearing a red cap with the supermarket logo.

I sighed.

He is saying, the woman behind me stepped up, that you are coming here three days in a row.

Thank you. Yes, it's true. Didn't supermarkets appreciate fidelity?

The man said something for his interpreter. She was politely sanctimonious, in perfect English. You are supposed to shop as rarely as possible. To reduce contagions.

The burly guardian nodded, his fever pistol in his hand. *Non è un passatempo!* he cried.

I was pleased to pick up the word *passatempo*. Perhaps my ear was tuning in. I pointed to my stick. I have a bad leg, I'm afraid. I can't carry much. I am shopping for a family of four.

The woman translated. The man lifted the pistol to my temple. He had never meant to keep me out. It was a question of asserting a certain mood. Ditto the policemen.

But what do you buy for three people without a stove? Possibly with dietary issues. Did my charges eat ham? The supermarket felt quite different with this task ahead of me. Cheese, but what cheese? I hesitated. What fruit? How much could I carry? Yogurts. Chocolate for the boy. Juice for the sick man. If he was. Hopefully they would make contact with the husband and be out already this afternoon. It might be useful to get some aspirin. I found a display with plasters, bandages and the like, but no medicines.

Aspirin? I asked a girl crouched to stack a low shelf. Her shirt was riding up her back, jeans cut low.

As-pi-rin.

Aspirina! Farmacia, Signore. Non supermercato! Farmacia.

Should I walk back the same way and risk passing the police again? Did I have the energy to drag my purchases

to the pharmacy? Apparently I did. Perhaps the servant's role suited me. For a moment I wondered why it
was impossible to imagine doing the same for my son's
family. Why did I have such a horror of being trapped in
their suburban house, their semi-detached atmosphere?
Most blameless is he, I remembered, centred in the sphere
of common duties. Or words to that effect.

Outside the pharmacy I had all the time in the world
to pursue these reflections. There were a dozen people
before me. Not in a queue exactly, but aware of who had
come first. I put down my bags and enjoyed the pale sunshine. Perhaps a father like Ulysses inevitably bred a dull
Telemachus. Life with Connie and me must always have
seemed precarious, imbalanced. Supposing, I almost said
out loud, you did become editor of the magazine. After
Dan. What would your mission be? A tram squealed by.
The sun gleamed on the polished window of the pharmacy
where I and other ghosts floated among cellulitis creams
and invitations to plump spectral lips with Fillerina. One
wanted to tell the truth, of course, but perhaps not the
truths that earnest people who buy such magazines want
to hear. That phase is over, I decided.

Aspirin, paracetamol, ibuprofen, sore-throat pastels,
cough syrup. I thought I might as well get anything useful.
Fortunately the police were no longer guarding the road.
Shuffling through the revolving doors of the hotel, I had a
special smile ready for the doorman, the younger of the two;
he shot me a puzzled look but didn't grasp the incongruity
of bulging supermarket bags. The world had changed so
much, so fast, nothing was expected to make sense.

By the time the knock came at the door I had found a cartoon channel on the TV. Expecting the boy. Instead it was her. She went straight past me to the bags, on the bed.

You are a good person, she said. Her quick hands sorted through the food. Then she remembered, Sir.

Call me, Frank, please. I hope I got enough.

Thank you.

Frank, I repeated. What is your name?

Her eyes glanced my way. I wondered if it was always the same mask, or if she managed to use fresh ones.

Any name will do, I said.

Perhaps she didn't understand this. It was curious how she was never quite still, always swaying a little, flexing. As if movement could protect her.

Just a name. To call you by.

She seemed puzzled.

Listen, I said, it's okay. I told her she had nothing to fear from me. I was leaving. Saturday morning. She should consider me at her disposal until then. A servant. A grandfather, if you like. Use the bathroom if you need it. Take a shower. Wash your clothes. Give the boy a bath. Let him sit down here and watch cartoons.

On the screen tiny children with mops of blue and orange hair were speaking in squeals.

No one is cleaning the rooms any more. Housekeeping has stopped checking. It's safe.

She watched me as I spoke. I realised that not being able to see a face one looks at the body more. She dropped the bags and went to the window.

Okay? She threw me an enquiring glance, then turned

130

the handle and stepped onto the balcony. I moved a little to see. She was looking over the parapet towards the entrance of the hotel. In the end it was a stroke of luck, I thought, to have this drama.

When I went out, I said, there was a man near the door. I thought he might be your husband.

She turned, touching her mask to check it was tight round her nose.

I was thinking, maybe you could take the SIM card out of your phone and put it in mine.

Her thoughts were elsewhere.

I repeated what I had said. Then you would have your numbers in my phone. You could call him.

She came back into the room, checking her watch. Thank you, she said. And hurried to the bags.

When you've finished the bottle of water just bring it down and fill it at the tap.

Thank you.

You still haven't given me a name.

She hesitated. Upstairs the thumping began.

Hakim.

Yes. She listened. It is . . . loud! Her voice was warmer, conversational. The skin wrinkled round the eyes. Then she moved to the door and stood for a moment checking the coast was clear.

XV

I lay on the bed. My knee had begun to throb, but I hadn't coughed or sneezed this morning. False alarms. I sat up, pulled off my trousers, explored the knee with my hands. It was swollen, but not huge. Flexing, there was a point where it clicked. Odd, I thought, how similar one's legs were to how they had been twenty or even thirty years ago. To look at, at least. It was the face that aged. And the hands.

How would Rachel's face have changed?

I lay back and blanked out for a while. What an odd dream of Dan that had been, beside me on the barge. I could feel Connie pressing, but it was easy to keep her at bay. Everything seemed easy this morning. There was something absurd about Connie, I thought. Like a belief abandoned years ago. Even the idea of losing half my savings seemed strangely irrelevant. You are waiting, I realised. What for? The little boy to come down? The woman again. I could give her a name myself, if she didn't want to oblige. Fatima, Zara. They were Arab names. But it seemed presumptuous. Where were these people from? I tried to imagine their lives. They had fled from Syria. A war zone.

Or Iraq. She was a nurse. Or she had a degree in Political Science. I realised I wanted her to be cultured and accomplished. Her husband a doctor or lawyer. They couldn't pursue their professions in Italy because of their illegal status. Or perhaps she had never done anything but clean rooms in luxury hotels. Her man worked on the metro, washed dishes. They had fled poverty in Algeria. Arriving in a boat. She spoke good French perhaps. They lived in a community of Arabs in some run-down part of Milan.

I was waiting for her to bring me another task. Or to send her boy to watch my television. We could look at an old Disney together. *The Little Mermaid* would take me back.

Had they come over to join her father? Or all together? Was there a mother? She had died during the crossing perhaps. It may be that the gulfs will wash us down. Ulysses seemed to look forward to it. Was the boy born here or there?

The minutes passed. It was strange she had not jumped at the chance to put her SIM card in my phone. I wondered if all SIM cards were compatible. I should have checked the make of her phone so I could buy another. I had seen that the mobile shops were open. People had to be able to communicate remotely; otherwise they would get together and infect each other.

I lapsed into a reverie of desert lives in brightly coloured robes. Crowded bazaars. A pitiless sun on flat roofs. Charming stereotypes. Though Dan had sent me on missions to Cairo and Damascus and Tunis. I knew what these cities were like. All our understanding had been shallow,

I thought. Our articles just arguments among ourselves, to see who got the better of whom. I began to wonder if I had ever done anything serious in my life, aside from nursing Rachel. Or trying to. Willing but clumsy. Accompanying her premature decay from one clinic to another. Stabbing needles in buttocks. The little revivals and false dawns, all the way to the revelation behind the grey door in Shimla. Grey-blue flesh on stone slab. The same mottling a child shrinks from in an old man's face. With the window beyond and the sunshine over the foreign town. Standing there looking out, with her body behind and the smell of death, not as bad as I had expected, and a world stretching dense and unknowable to distant peaks. Every experience opens a view to some new departure. I saw all this again, lying on my bed in the Grand Hotel Milano, with the clarity and serenity of a waking dream. You are washed up like a bone on a beach, I thought. And I thought, Time for lunch!

All meals were in the Breakfast Room now. We were to eat on plastic plates, queuing a metre apart from each other up to the counter where three waiters served behind pans and tureens, amid powerful smells of disinfectant. At no point would any skin touch anything that any other skin had touched. I turned round with my veal cutlet and saw the woman of the odd couple eating alone. On impulse, with a naturalness that surprised me, I limped to her table and asked if I could sit with her. She seemed dazed, but didn't say no. I put down my tray, propped up my stick, removed my mask.

Difficult to know where to put these things!

She half smiled, biting her lower lip. Perhaps she hadn't understood. I sat down and began to eat. She had finished her food and could easily have stood up and gone. Or put her mask on if she was worried. Instead she stayed, looking pensively right and left. She had full cheeks, clouded eyes.

I saw the scene at the door this morning, I said. When they didn't let you out.

Ah. She winced. Later, for . . . medicine, I am gone. Out.

Good. I'm glad. I hesitated. Your husband is not well?

On the table her hand had clenched round her napkin. Yes, she said.

I'm sorry.

She pulled a face that told me she was used to this and worse.

I finished my food slowly, occasionally glancing up. Our eyes met.

Caffè?

Thank you.

She took her tray to the counter, carrying a dazed look about her. Quite the opposite of the Arab woman, always so urgently focused.

Plastic cups, I sighed when she came back.

She smiled. Five-star plastic.

It was exactly the remark Rachel would have made.

What is your name?

When she narrowed her eyes you could see a dusting of freckles on the skin beneath.

Carmen.

*

Hakim came some time after three. He was gloomy and stern and made it clear his duty was to watch the front of the hotel from my balcony. He hurried out there. But I found some cartoons on the TV and he came to stand at the French windows to watch. I moved the armchair to a position where I could see him and the cartoons together. Wouldn't it really have been wiser, I wondered, and perhaps better for them in the end, if I had let the hotel management know at once? Pushing past me at the door, the boy definitely had a smell about him. I calculated there were sixty hours till I left the hotel for good.

Hakim went back and forth. Crouching down to press his head between the fancy stone supports of the balcony, craning to look at the TV from the window. The cartoons seemed to be Japanese but the voices were squeaky Italian. A girl clutched a sparkling crystal with magical powers. Hakim's lips moved as he watched. Then frowned when he saw me watching him. He rushed back to his observation post. I worried he must be getting cold out there in just his T-shirt. The day had clouded over and was spotting rain.

I got down on my knees, carefully, opened the minibar and retrieved the Godiva chocolates. Hadn't the good lady ridden naked to help the poor in some way? I couldn't remember the story. I hopped out to the balcony. Gourmet Truffles, the box said. Hakim was circumspect, picking at the gold wrapping with dirty nails. A helicopter rumbled above. Then his eyes widened over the chocolate. He might have been a cartoon himself. He even rubbed a hand on his stomach and yummed.

May I have one, perhaps?

He didn't understand.

One? I held up a finger, pointed to the box, to my lips.

Nam! he cried and his thin arm thrust the box at me.

Back in my chair, mouth full of truffle, I began to cry. Rubbing a sleeve across my face, I caught the boy's eyes, at the door, watching me now rather than the cartoon. A picture of perplexity, mouth dribbling chocolate. And I started to laugh, shaking my head, still crying. His puzzlement brightened to a smile, then a glare, and once more he returned to his sentry duty.

I relaxed. The wave that had boiled over me was draining away. Perhaps it was just a reaction to being locked up like this. For some reason I thrust a hand down the side of the armchair cushion, as if to recover a lost tissue, and fished up a piece of foil: Durex Real Feel. I pushed it back, relieved the boy hadn't seen. But cheered too. What are luxury hotels for in the end?

Baba! the boy cried. He ran to the window, looked at me as if expecting to find his mother, seemed disconcerted, ran back out again. Baba! Baba! He was yelling over the parapet. Then he hared through the room out of the door and away.

So that's it, I thought. The husband had come. I went to the bathroom and washed my face. Good. Then hurried to the balcony myself and looked down. White taxis, black limousine. Here and there a driver by his vehicle. The air was cold and damp. I waited. Would Hakim and his mother simply walk out of the hotel and embrace Baba? What about the sick man? The cat? Their things?

There must, I realised, be some service entrance. An underground garage. A service lift. They would meet there.

But who cared? They were gone. You wouldn't want them back, I thought. All the same I was still watching the front door of the hotel from my sixth-floor balcony. I put on my coat, picked up cigarettes and Tennyson and dragged the chair outside. I wanted to see them again. Though I knew I wouldn't see them.

I read something called The Lotos-Eaters, glancing up every few lines. Happy islanders lure stranded sailors into narcotic oblivion. I lit a cigarette. All things have rest, and ripen toward the grave. A minibus arrived at the hotel and a group of men climbed out. Chinese perhaps. It was hard to see. The doormen came out to assist with the bags. There was a busy milling.

We have had enough of action, the sailors decide, Roll'd to starboard, roll'd to larboard. The cigarette had me coughing. At their disposal, I thought, I had understandably been disposed of. All things are taken from us, and become / Portions and parcels of the dreadful past. Referring everything you read, I once told Rachel, to your own life, is a form of madness. Is there any other way to read? she asked. But that was before she fell ill.

Anyway, I was alone again. I went inside, turned on the TV and watched through the afternoon. CNN, BBC, Fox, Sky. I put myself at their mercy. Clearly, I decided, great upheavals and modern media were made for each other. All the better an upheaval that locked people up alone with TV or computer in a state of fear. Same information repeated over and over. On every channel. More and more urgently. A stronger narcotic than the lotos. Without the happy effects. Apparently there were some who denied the emergency, but they were mad or evil. The disease drifted invisible in the air. It clung to familiar surfaces. It rose up in exponential curves. Emptying streets. Filling mortuaries.

Why am I not afraid? I thought. I was only afraid of succumbing to these emphatic voices.

But now I had turned the TV on, I couldn't turn it off. I had to expose myself to the onslaught. Diet and virus. Public transport and virus. Sex and virus. Somebody had thrown a party, walked on a beach, touched her nose under her mask. Air travel was dead. An opportunity to save the planet.

Again I thought of Dan's magazine. Did the job interest me? I imagined bringing the staff together for the first editorial meeting. Okay, my friends, what is the thing we want to say, we really need to say, but for some reason can't say, or don't say? That was the question I used to throw at my Plain Speech team. Once someone answered, EVERYONE SHUT UP! and we all laughed.

A man was standing outside a cemetery in Bergamo. Not so far from here. Beside a stack of coffins. I opened the minibar and poured myself a cognac.

Dear Deborah, at the funeral everyone spoke of Dan's heroism, working all hours to the very day he died, but is that really what the old should be doing? Even Lancelot passed his last years in a monastery.

Fantasy conversations.

A young Australian woman, in Seoul, enthused about oriental discipline. For Sky. The Koreans, she said, put aside selfishness, privacy, individualism, in the name of the common good.

I rolled the fiery liquor round my mouth.

What was old age about, then? I wondered. Avoiding death? Even while knowing death must come. Threescore years and ten. Fourscore. Five. Being old in order to be older? Taking presents to Sophie on her fifth birthday. Her fifteenth. Her twenty-fifth.

Dear Charles, confident as I am that you will get the job, this must surely be the first question to address: old age. I would be happy to write such a piece for you, if you are interested.

Or giving Sophie the example of my dying? Getting her used to the idea. Was that it? Your death her birthday present.

It occurred to me I might ask Reception to put a call through to Alberto Rizzo's room. Could we discuss this stuff together?

He would say old age was about spending as much time as possible with Carmen.

I drained the cognac. For years, I thought, you have lived alone without the word loneliness so much as crossing your mind. What had set off this new need? I remembered those moments at lunch, eating while the Sicilian woman sat opposite. It was frustrating not speaking the same language. But a pleasure to be speechlessly close. Then Hakim catching me crying. His mother's eyes between mask and headscarf in the attic.

Old age a presence that allows youth to be aware of itself. Was that it?

One retreats to a monastery, of course, to prepare one's soul for the end.

A whole generation has been lost, a journalist was telling us from a village in Spain. I rummaged in the minibar and, setting aside the whisky for some moment of dire need, opened the port. Graham's No.5. Nineteen per cent proof. Forty per cent of the over eighties, the journalist said. Gone. But surely, I spoke up, a lost generation is one that dies young, not old. I was arguing with the media again, and finding the port predictably sickly. The journalist paid no attention. I saw Rachel shaking her head. More people than in the war, he insisted. As if this were a magic number. I stood up and shouted: How can I be part of a lost generation when my life is already lived?

I had known this would happen. I sat down. What does Ben really think of me? I wondered. You're Sophie's grandfather, Dad. A role. Hence my duty: stay alive. So Sophie can know my old age. The TV had turned its attention to those evil governments who hid the real death toll. Perhaps it was something I could discuss with Connie. Relationships with children and grandchildren. Not that I had any desire to discuss this with her. Or anything else. Then I thought it might be interesting to sit in silence with Connie, over a meal. To see how that felt. To sit quietly with Connie and feel the weight of all that once had been between us. Rachel and I were often together in silence. Working or walking. Over a desk or side by side. But to be with Connie was to be talking to Connie. Talked at by Connie. Our relationship a delight of battle. War of words. We would need to fall from the Tower of Babel, I thought.

To forget each other's language. I imagined Connie and me meeting again and finding our words made no sense, we couldn't score points.

What does it mean to prepare one's soul?

I sipped the port, switching between the channels as between competing toxicities. PPE was an acronym I hadn't heard before. A tale of little meaning though the words are strong. That was how it looked to the lotoseaters. I doubted Alberto would want to discuss this. Deprived of the operation that would give him more time with Carmen.

Would she be alone again at dinner?

You want to tell Carmen about Rachel. Of course. I got to my feet; I felt shaky and befuddled. The mortality rate was not the same as the fatality rate, CNN explained. You are planning to confront this grieving woman with your own grief. Of old. It was that evening with Deborah set this all off. At the same time I felt gloriously indifferent. I saw myself from a cool distance plunging into corridors in search of a woman who would not understand a word I said. And this calm observation of my folly – looking down on the scene from the sixth floor – only inflamed the craving to be on the move, to tell my story. Shake the balloon from the trees, find Carmen. Know Carmen. Anyone. And the more distinct and urgent that craving became, like the need to pee, so the more calmly and indifferently I observed it, with the sickly taste of the Graham's No.5 in my mouth.

All things ripen toward the grave. In silence.

I silenced CNN, found my stick and stumbled to the door.

Perhaps it was Tennyson's fault, I reflected on the stairs. Poetry should be banned. There were twenty-eight stairs per floor. Two flights of fourteen steps. I climbed down, wince by wince, not in respect of the rules, but to sober up. Six times twenty-eight. Perhaps all my walking these last ten years – countless miles of city streets – had been a way of putting off this question: what is old age for? Now that the illusion of doing things is gone. Or making things. Helping. Even saying things. There is nothing to say. That is the truth. The voices on CNN were a chorus of crickets, I thought. It would have been good to have made that observation to Dan. BBC: June bugs. Fox News: cicadas. Insect clamour in the dog days. At best you threw a different buzz into the mix. But now I realised I was curious to check out the garage and the service exit. Not because I expected to see my Arab family again, but just . . . because.

There was no garage. The basement had the gym, a swimming pool, sauna, Turkish bath, Business Centre. All closed. And storage rooms. Presumably. Locked doors. SOLO AUTORIZZATI. The ceilings were lower. The corridors narrower. No one around. No prints on the walls. The background hum louder. A generator? I pressed my masked nose to the glass and gazed at an empty pool. How we could have enjoyed ourselves! And as I came out into a large, malodorous depot where a big iron shutter rolled up at the back of the hotel, two delivery men were pulling something from the back of a van parked in the rainy street. Under the supervision of a janitor. I watched from a distance. They walked it into the building between lines of bins, a long heavy box.

XVI

Eight p.m. In the Breakfast Room there were open windows. It was chilly. The odd couple were not there. Who was the *cercueil* for? No doubt hotel managers were trained to deal with these eventualities. I ate risotto, again, opened the email, saw Deborah's name, then the battery died.

Round the room the guests were keeping their coats on. The Hasidic family in black. Miss West Coast had a fur collar, opposite her beau in *pardessus gris*. I wished them well. One elderly man was sitting right under the open window. At which point, out of the blue, it occurred to me that I had written Power of Good just a month or two after Rachel's diagnosis. Why was I thinking of this now? All the examples I had quoted – the fierce competition for militant rectitude – came out of my experience at the Institute. But the anger that was to make me a pariah had to do with Rachel. How had I not seen this before?

I put my fork down and sipped Cabernet. When a young person dies there is anger. People had been surprised by my ferocity. Hate speech, someone said. Was it possible, I wondered, that the old were so reluctant to die because the upright young had packed them off to so-called homes, no longer wanted to watch them doing what old folk have to do, grow decrepit? I shall die *before my grandfather*, Rachel protested. The thought drove her mad. The man was in his late nineties, adrift in the doldrums of dementia.

I could never see what difference the fate of others made to one's own, and she could not see how I could not see.

Perhaps the grandfather was a proxy for me.

What about the man in the attic? I thought.

Limping to the buffet to grab a sweet – there was strawberry cheesecake – I had the bizarre desire to re-dream the dream with Dan. Continue our conversation. Where did we suppose we were going on that barge? You must call it a day, Dan. Having yourself buried next to a lover you never lived with is a form of denial. As if life could be lived after death. Or something preserved. A sparkling sword for the eyes of future museumgoers. It's over. Toss the pen in the bin.

Still here? Madam Business was waiting for the lift. In bulky blue trouser suit, red nose poking over surgical mask.

I have a flight Saturday.

Ah, fingers crossed! She seemed rather jolly this evening.

Yourself?

Too much still to do here, I'm afraid.

I didn't ask what. In the lift she said she thought by now we were the only ones left on the sixth floor. From worrying about the price of the rooms we would soon be able to put in an option to purchase the place.

Every catastrophe an opportunity!

She filled her mask with laughter.

Could I speak to Alberto Rizzi? I'm afraid I don't have his room number, no.

This line is busy, sir.

Dear Frank, Deborah had written – I put the phone on charge – I have the impression things are going to get seriously bad here and have decided to head home while it's still possible. I'll be passing through the station in Milan Saturday morning. If you're still around we might grab a coffee and talk about the magazine after Dan.

I stood on the balcony for a while, listening to sirens, enjoying the breezy damp of the evening. Hakim had spilled Godiva Gold by the railing. I wiped a little grit from a last praline and ate it. Your leg gets worse, I thought, but you cannot be still. Leaning on my stick, I left my room and once again climbed to the attic.

He was indeed still there. Easing the door ajar, I became aware of a sound as of undertow on shingle. And the now familiar fetor. I should go down at once and inform Reception.

I stepped into the darkness. The breathing came in slow waves. Rising and falling. Like the sea in a cave.

Is anyone there? Can I come in?

Yes. The reply was prompt, throaty. Please. There was a sharp cough.

I've come to help, but I'm afraid I can't see.

One moment.

After a few seconds the lamp came on. Everything was as it had been. I picked my way through the clutter, circling round the dusty boxes. Into the den. There were two mattresses and a heap of blankets and bathrobes. The ceiling slanted low. The light was dim but unpleasantly white. Two buckets were covered with cardboard. Food and bottles on a cloth. He was lying along the wall, the lamp just beyond his head. The cat blinked beside him.

You are English, yes? He had raised himself a little on his elbows. Our eyes met.

Where is your daughter? The boy?

I wanted to crouch. My knee wouldn't bend.

He coughed again. Rania is not my daughter.

I looked more carefully. He was in his sixties. Perhaps. Cheeks sallow, but with a strong unshaven mouth.

You're not well. Do you have a fever?

He put a hand on the cat. The animal purred, as though the circumstances were entirely satisfactory.

Is it getting worse? Better?

He half smiled. Not better.

We should get you to hospital.

No. He rolled on his side and coughed again. Rania will come.

When?

He put a hand over his face and rubbed his forehead.

Headache?

I shifted the lamp a little further from him, turned my back against the wall and, holding tight to my stick, slid down till I was sitting on the floor close to his head, bad

147

leg stretched rigid in front of me. The low lamp threw long shadows. The smell seemed stronger here, but also more intimate.

You are the man who brought the food.

Yes. After a few moments, I asked, Do you know if her husband has found a place? A flat?

He didn't reply and I thought he might be sleeping. I rested my own head against the wall and gazed around. A suitcase was spilling clothes. By the mattress, half hidden under a blanket, was a book. He drew a deeper breath and again there was a sound as of water over pebbles. A sea surge. I manoeuvred my stick and used the hilt to pull the book towards me. A paperback with a simple white cover.

He cleared his throat. I must thank you for your kindness – what is your name?

Apparently he was wide awake. I told him. And yours? Where are you from?

Egypt. Long ago. My name is Omar. You are here on business?

A funeral.

Ah. Without opening his eyes an expression of pained sympathy crossed his face. Bad luck. A loved one?

I hesitated. Yes.

Bad luck, he repeated. I'm sorry.

The minutes passed. Against the wall, my back was growing stiff and cold. Some sensible decision was required. But what? I leafed through the book. The text was curiously arranged in blocks of ten or fifteen lines with a ragged margin to the left. The corner of one page had been folded over twice. The Arabic script seemed marvellously fluid.

Listen, I suggested, if I knew your situation, perhaps I could be more useful.

He pulled an arm from under the blankets and reached blindly behind him in my direction.

Give me your hand, sir.

I did. Mine icy, his feverish.

Rania will come soon, he said.

She didn't come. I was aware it might be unwise now to touch my face with the hand that had held his. I must be on guard against myself – my habit of poking a finger into the corner of an eye. At the same time, despite the chill and the fetor, I felt relaxed. Drugged almost.

This was dangerous. I struggled to my feet, pressing on Excalibur. The cat opened an eye. I shuffled about in the tight space, poking at things with the stick. A toy truck. A pair of fluffy slippers. Rania – the name didn't seem to fit the person – had heaped underwear and shirts in neat piles on the boxes. A roll of toilet paper. With the light on the floor behind, my shadow lurched ahead, hunched and clumsy. Just leave, I decided. Not reporting these people was already a favour. There was a broom and dustpan beside a heap of dirt at the point where the ceiling came down too low to stand. Beyond, the dust looked thick.

I went back to his mattress and lowered myself against the wall. His breathing was louder. I noticed recurring clicks and wheezes. The cat settled down. And after some minutes, in the most natural way possible, the creature began to explain that his name was Farooq, he had worked

as a ship's cat and disembarked in Genoa. He grinned
Hakim's grin, licked a paw. You can read it in his book!
Now he hunted mice for the Five Star Alliance. They were
hung in the pantry and served in the rooftop restaurant.
But how can I make ends meet for only five cents a mouse?
Suddenly the animal scampered away. There was a tink-
ling splash. I shook my head. Omar was kneeling by one
of the buckets. Back curved. He was wearing a red fleece.
Jeans. He covered the bucket and moved crab-like back
to bed.

Why not come to my room? I said.

He shivered, pulling the blankets on top of him. The
cat patted a paw on the wool.

You could use the bathroom. Sleep in a bed. It's warm.

Again he was slow to answer. And you, Frank?

There are armchairs.

He started to cough. When it went on he pulled the
blankets over his head. The coughs continued, muffled
by the covers. Then stopped. He didn't pull his head out.

I couldn't decide whether I was relieved he hadn't
accepted my offer. Perhaps he might still accept it. I
watched the slight rise and fall of the blanket. The really
noble thing to do would be to carry the slop buckets down
to my bathroom and empty them. Of course there was no
way I could do this, on the stairs, with my bad knee.

I fell into a kind of reverie again, exploring old thoughts
in the dim light of this new situation. Why did I want to
do something noble? Again my mind was drawn back to
those last flare-ups with Rachel. You're not thinking of me,
just how fucking sensitive you're being! She apologised.

We had never argued. Suffering is attractive, I thought; you have a chance to shine. Take your seat at the Round Table and enjoy the glow. Perhaps I became attached to her illness. You don't even see me any more, she said.

Do you have children, Frank?

I opened my eyes and saw he had emerged from the bedclothes.

A son, and a granddaughter. And you? When he didn't reply, I added, Omar?

He chuckled. Four. Three sons. A daughter.

Brave man. Where are they?

Clearing his throat, he began to talk. Layla was in Alexandria. She did not want to come to Europe. She had not married. Gamal and Hassan were in Bari. The twins. They work where they can. You understand? He hesitated. I can trust you, Frank?

Yes.

When you don't have the right papers it is not easy to move around.

I imagine.

Rania will bring a doctor, he said. His voice was gravelly, low. God willing, it is nothing.

And the other son? Your wife?

He was silent. Again I wondered what time it was. I had neither watch nor phone with me. Faintly, through the thick walls of the old hotel, came the wail of a siren.

Do you have a spare blanket?

Of course! Now he answered at once. With a grunt, he raised himself on an elbow and reached for something folded over his feet.

I don't want to deprive you.

He didn't reply. I draped the blanket over my baldness, wriggled it between my shoulders and the wall. I was surprised what a pleasure this was. How cosy it felt to be inside the warm wool. Like a monk in his cowl.

Where did you learn English?

In a hotel. In Napoli. Where I worked, many years, until my wife died. Her name was Farah.

I said I was sorry.

That was the beginning of our troubles. When we took her to hospital.

Ah. Who was we? I asked.

Me and my other son. The oldest. Khalil. Then he said, Rania's husband.

I wanted him to go on, but perhaps talking was tiring.

You know what Khalil means? In Arabic.

I didn't.

Friend.

Nice.

Instead I should call him my enemy! He laughed bitterly, which set off his coughing.

Why?

He shook his head. I don't want to talk about Khalil.

For a long time I stared into the shadows and bric-a-brac of the attic, then must have slept. When I woke the light was off. It was pitch-dark. His breathing was louder. Suddenly I felt extremely anxious. My neck was stiff. I needed to pee. You are a fool. I fumbled to my right, found the lamp, felt for the switch.

Rania was sitting on the floor beside him. Her chin

twitched as she quickly drew her scarf across her face. But I had seen. She had a dark bruise on her left cheek. A wound of some sort at its centre. She turned and when she turned back she was masked. Hakim was stretched on the floor behind.

Hello, I said.

Hello, sir.

Omar said you were bringing a doctor.

Tomorrow.

His breathing is bad.

She nodded.

I looked at her. Why not bring him down to my room? He will be warm.

For a few moments she swayed back and forth, cross-legged. She seemed to think with her body.

Okay, she said.

PART THREE

XVII

So now I am a nurse again. Of sorts. Omar is in my bed. I have helped him to the bathroom. Washed his underwear. Administered aspirin and cough syrup. We do not have a thermometer, but every hour or so I place a hand on his forehead, compare it with mine. Through the afternoon his fever rises. He is drifting in and out of sleep, sweating profusely. I keep his water glass filled, listen to his breathing.

None of this is like nursing Rachel. There is no death sentence. I haven't abandoned a career to look after him. I never adored his body. Yet little things take me back. Plumping pillows. Bringing pills. The combination of tension and boredom.

I have spread his underwear and socks on the parapet of the balcony. There's a clear cold sky today. The plaza outside the station is empty, the Alps visible on the horizon. Gazing that way, I wonder was it wise, all that travel we did years ago? We meant to turn illness into a love story. A romantic journey. And it did bring exquisite intimacy. But threw us back entirely on each other. Not for brief months, but long years. For years there was only

157

us, the illness and an end that seemed darker the more it receded.

Back in the room it's a pleasure finding Omar's head on the creamy pillows, Hakim sprawled on the rug. As if I were finally getting value for money. The boy has spent the day watching cartoons. And running. He races back and forth between the door and the French windows. Dodging armchairs and coffee table. TV to one side, bed to the other. I hope no one is in the room beneath. His bare feet thump. He stops and jumps on the spot, black hair flopping. Or he scowls at the television, shooting from an index finger. Pow! Blam! Getting into the battle. The cartoons are always battles. Evil powers and good genies. This is the only way of conceiving the world. Humanity is in an almighty war against the virus, says Fox News.

Omar does not seem the combative sort. He doesn't complain about the boy's exuberance. Sometimes Hakim rushes to him, clasps his head tight, then rushes off. Both put their trust entirely in Rania. She organises and decides. But Rania went out early this morning to find a doctor. How will she get him into the hotel? I asked. Omar shook his head. I took the withered tulips from the low table and put them in the bathroom waste bin, moved the vase out of the boy's way. The cat is shut out on the balcony. I will have to work out what to do about the shit.

At breakfast there was comedy. I had stacked my tray and was ready to fill my pockets with food when Carmen came to sit at my table. Her eyes were smiling, her hair freshly washed. Her white mask seemed no more than a party tease. I could only think how astonished she would be at the four croissants on my plate. The apples and yogurts. I tried to drape a napkin over them.

Good morning. She hung her bag on the chair. She was wearing a skirt.

And Alberto?

She placed her hands on the table and leaned forward a little. Having my mask off, I drew back. She seemed not to notice.

Ospedale!

The operation?

She nodded.

Today?

She shook her head.

Tomorrow?

She nodded again. Her eyes were full of life.

I am so pleased for you, I said.

When she went to the buffet I stuffed the food into my pockets right and left, not even checking whether any staff were looking. And through the whole of our silent meal together I was thinking that if I infected her and she infected Alberto on his return from hospital I could be the instrument of his death.

All the same, standing to leave I asked: Let me know when you have news.

Her forehead wrinkled. Lunch?

One o'clock?

She smiled. I noticed a crumb at the corner of her mouth. It did not seem she was wearing make-up.

Rania keeps her mask on at all times. She knows I saw her face but isn't going to say anything about it. During the night, going to the bathroom, I peeked. She was in the bed with Omar, the boy snuggled between. But there was barely light to see and she had her wounded cheek to the pillow. Now, returning from breakfast, I found her gone. The boy was watching television. I wondered where she had been with him yesterday evening when I found Omar alone. Was there a doctor in the hotel? She had said herself that if she went out she couldn't get back in.

I asked Omar. He nibbled at his croissant, but his throat was sore. I propped him on cushions to eat some yogurt. Hakim gobbled two croissants.

Perhaps she uses the service door, I said. At the back of the hotel. Is that how you came in?

The sick man shook his head, more as if trying to free himself from some pain than in reply. In the daylight I could see his cheeks were pockmarked. He was suffering, but I did not get the impression he was anxious. Rania did all the worrying. Checking the phone, I opened an email from Ben telling me I really must get WhatsApp; it was so much easier to share photos and videos. He included three pictures taken on a visit to an adventure park. One in particular struck me. A threesome selfie, at the edge of a pond with ducks. It was the expression on my son's face that caught my attention. A certain tilt of the jaw, a cut of the lips.

I went to the bathroom to shave. Some thoughts should never be allowed to surface. I studied my own face in the mirror. They bring only poison. I had years ago set aside any speculation that Ben might be Dan's child. I never challenged Connie. Rachel was scathing of the notion one lived on in one's children. What kind of consolation was that? What kind of a prison for the children? Yet Ben's glance as he pulled wife and daughter into the photo frame, crouching among the ducks, was exactly Giles Cleverley's when he stood beside the grave and spoke of Lady Cleverley the poet and Dan Sandow the editor.

I shaved calmly. I enjoy the neat lines as the razor takes off strips of foam and beard. The skin glistens, the face is discovered anew. I have a wider mouth than my son's, a paler skin. I remembered the pointed nose in the coffin. That twist of the lips. Had there been a smell of camphor? I rinsed off, sat on the edge of the bathtub and studied the photo again. Sophie was overdoing the happy child's pose. Her mother seemed distant and preoccupied. What could it add, I thought, or take away from my life at this point to know whose genes were whose?

More pertinent was the question, what if my guests were lying to me? Back in the room I went to the desk, found my passport and ticket printout and slipped them into the inside pocket of my jacket. Aside from the contents of my wallet, safely in my trouser pocket, it was hard to see what they could steal. Perhaps tonight I should use the room's wall safe. But with luck my guests would be gone by then. There was only so much they could take from the minibar.

Omar wasn't lying about his illness. You couldn't fake that breathing, hour after hour, or the drifting in and out of sleep. As with Rachel, sickness became the one certainty. I moved the desk chair to sit beside him.

Would you like your book?

No thanks, Frank.

Too tired?

My head.

I had something of a headache myself after the night in the armchair.

What is it about? I asked.

He turned and met my eyes. He seemed pleased. The waters of old Egypt, he said.

The Nile?

When Egypt was great. He reflected. When other peoples were . . . jealous. Because of Egypt's waters.

I couldn't think of anything to say. The morning passed. The boy ran back and forth, occasionally demanding attention. I had held back a last croissant. If they stayed until evening I would have to find more food.

It talks about waters and farming. Omar was suddenly speaking again. Perhaps he had dozed off. Gardens, plants. Where paradise was.

I didn't get it. Was the book esoteric, historical, or what?

I was never any good with plants, I said.

There was a knock on the door. I got to my feet. Rania. But maybe not. The knock came again sharply. Hakim! I nodded to the bathroom. Someone was using a passepartout. The lock whirred. The boy moved in a flash. The handle turned. I had engaged the privacy chain. The door banged against it. Sorry, sir, came the voice.

Yes. One moment.

I have come to change the towels and empty the bins.

I fixed my mask and spoke through the gap. I would prefer not to have anyone in my room, thank you. I am leaving Saturday morning.

And the minibar, sir?

I have everything I need.

Hakim was crouched in the shower. It's okay, I said. He's gone now. The boy rushed past me and jumped on the bed beside his grandfather. I asked Omar for the name of the author of his book and typed it into Google, but nothing came up.

Do you read a lot?

He shook his head. Rania had found the book in a room. A guest had left it. He read newspapers in cafes, and watched the news.

Al Jazeera?

Again he shook his head.

I'm sorry you had to leave your flat, I said. Rania told me. A landlord like that should be put in jail.

Beside him the boy was nagging. Omar said something in Arabic. The boy whined. I remembered a small success with Sophie that had brought me a scolding from Ben. Do you like games, Hakim? I found the app on my phone and handed it to him. His mood changed instantly. He sat up on the pillow and bent his head over it, fingers stabbing.

Omar spoke to him and began to cough. Eventually I said: Rania has a bruise on her face.

Hearing his mother's name the boy glanced up.

A bruise, a wound.

It is shameful, Omar sighed. We have had some trouble. But Khalil is not a bad person.

It looked serious to me.

Omar closed his eyes. The boy went back to his game. We were silent for a few minutes. Then Omar pulled himself on his elbows and took a sip of water. You have been married, Frank, he cleared his throat. You have a son, a granddaughter. We live in a hard situation here. Now this sickness makes it worse. My son – he sipped at the water - he wants to return, to Egypt. Rania will not go. For Hakim.

I watched him. Seen practically, I thought, their story was of no more importance to me than the truth about my son's genes. Or the future of Dan's magazine. Or The Passing of Arthur. What mattered to me was to be on my flight on Saturday. And to get my knee seen to. Yet I had put myself at their disposal.

In the boy's hands my phone trilled a little tune of triumph. He punched the air and showed the screen to Omar. You win! he shouted. In English. Then settled down again. Omar smiled. Rania wants him to grow up here.

I smiled back. I liked his gentle manner. Actually, I said, I was married twice, Omar. Getting from the first wife to the second was hard. You know? Like crossing the desert. I laughed. Then everything was fine.

Why had I said this? He put down the glass and sank back on the pillows. He had a strong forehead, prominent nose, lean shoulders. I had the impression of a man with deep reserves, alert to what was going on around him, but not at all reactive. He hadn't once complained.

A good marriage is a wonderful thing, Frank, he said.

Yes. I struggled with a rush of emotion. Everything is easy.

That's right. He nodded.

I made an effort to calm myself, to keep things light. Even when you disagree, I said, somehow you agree. And wherever you eat, the food is good.

It is true! His eyes brightened. People are kind to you. Even officials. Even the police!

We both laughed. Then it must be love, I said.

And now, Frank?

She died. We are both widowers, Omar.

He frowned. We are both alive, he said. Then he asked, You are not afraid of this illness, Frank?

I thought about it. I suppose I should be. But for some reason I'm not.

The phone interrupted us. The hotel phone. It was the first time I had heard it ring.

Omar spoke to Hakim. He sounded grittier in Arabic. The boy paused his game.

A voice told me that partial settlement of my account was required.

I am leaving on Saturday.

We need partial settlement for bills over 3,000 euros, sir.

Omar coughed and quickly hid his face in the pillow. To pay online, the voice was saying, I could follow the steps described on the TV selecting Automatic Checkout. Or I could settle at the desk in Reception.

After lunch, I said.

Rania arrived as I was preparing to go down to eat. Her knock was soft. I released the security chain. A short, slim woman stood beside her, Chinese I thought. Grey trousers and green anorak. She wore a mask and transparent plastic visor. A white cap to cover her hair. Blue rubber gloves. She did not immediately come into the room but spoke in Italian to Rania.

She asks that you wear a mask, Rania told me. Also we must open the window.

I did as I was told. Rania hurried to find a mask for Hakim. The doctor held the door open to create a current. Since I had turned the heating up, the fresh air rolled in chill and damp. The cat scampered across the room and out into the corridor.

Bibi!

Hakim shot after it, pushing by the doctor, ignoring his mother's cry. There was a moment's confusion. I made to go after the boy but was pulled up by my knee. Rania said something to the doctor and hurried out. I was left wincing, shaking my head. I will be late for Carmen, I thought.

The doctor came in. She opened her bag on the desk, then talked to Omar from the foot of the bed. Both spoke Italian. Both voices were matter-of-fact. Coming round the bed she pointed her thermometer gun; with rubber gloves and visor she looked like something in a cartoon. He extended an arm and she moved close enough to attach a blood pressure device, averting her face. When he coughed, she turned and walked out onto the balcony. Rania came back with the boy, but without the cat. When she closed the door the doctor called to her and she opened it again. There was a steady draught. Hakim was whining, tugging his mother's arm. I could have been watching *La traviata*, I thought, sipping champagne.

Now Omar lifted his fleece. His back was spectacularly hairy. The doctor unrolled a thin plastic sheet over his skin and slid the stethoscope up and down. He breathed deeply. At last she stepped back and went to the bathroom taking her bag. A tap came on.

Where is the cat? I asked.

Rania rolled her eyes. An expression I hadn't expected at all. Ironic, almost flirtatious.

How did you get her in the hotel? At the back?

The doctor reappeared and came to stand at the foot of the bed. She spoke quietly to Rania and Omar together. Both asked questions. The boy fretted and turned to look at me. I was watching from the armchair, thinking Carmen would already be at table. Hakim opened his eyes wide in an appeal for help. To get the cat? Rania reached in her pocket and produced a purse.

I'll pay. I got to my feet. Rania shook her head, pulling out notes.

Please, let me. I broke your phone. How much is it? I addressed the doctor.

One hundred euros, she said. In good English. I pulled out my wallet. Omar struggled up on his elbows and started speaking urgently to Rania.

No, she told me.

Please, I insist.

Frank! Omar sighed from the cushions. We are already in your debt.

I broke your phone.

167

Rania counted out the notes. You fell, she said in her strange high voice. It is not your fault.

The doctor waited. Behind her visor. There was something very definite about her small erect figure. As if science had shorn her of all ambiguity. She put the money in a pouch at her waist.

You have a problem with your knee, she said to me.

I fell on it. A few days ago.

Is it swollen?

It was. Now it's just a bit puffy.

How did you fall?

Forwards. Bang on the knee.

It hurts all the time or when you walk?

When I put weight on it.

She seemed to be trying to decide whether to examine it or not.

You will need an X-ray. Possibly you have a fractured patella. You must see a specialist. Unfortunately this is not a good moment.

I understand.

Here you must wear a mask at all times. Okay? Change it every three hours. Change the air here every fifteen minutes. Wash your hands frequently. Isolate yourself from all persons outside your family group for fourteen days.

I was astonished that she had said family group. Will he be okay? I asked. But Rania was already leading the doctor away. Please, she turned to me, make sure Hakim stays in the room.

The boy rushed to the door. I stood with my back to it. He launched himself at the handle. Bibi, he whined. I

168

inserted the privacy chain, which was beyond his reach. He burst into tears, pummelling me with his fists. Out of view, Omar was calling from the bed. The boy was beside himself, a fury of flashing eyes and dishevelled hair. Then he sank to the floor sobbing. I felt bewildered, transported. I crouched and touched his shoulder. You need to eat, Hakim, I said.

XVIII

I got down to the Breakfast Room at two. Rania had
returned after some fifteen minutes. There were still bread,
cheese and apples for them. I hurried along the corridor
with my stick, ignoring the pain, hoping Carmen would
still be at table. Beside the lift a notice had appeared, in
English. Forbidden Descent. I pressed the call button.

Sir!

I was intercepted as I stepped out of the doors. It was
the young woman – dark hair tugged into a ponytail –
who hadn't wanted to give me an *autodichiarazione*.
When I pointed to the stick – I am on the sixth floor, you
understand – she said, Please, come this way, sir. Behind
the Plexiglas screen she consulted with her older colleague.
Given the cancellations, sir, there are premium suites available on the first floor. My phone rang while she was talking. Not a name but a number. 212. The New York area
code. I refused the call. This would be more luxurious than
my present accommodation, the receptionist purred, but
the management was happy to offer me the same price.
In the interests of containing the epidemic. I said I did not
want to be exposed to a new environment. Given my age I

was at high risk. In that case, sir, I am afraid you will have to use the stairs.

I was hurrying away when her colleague called me back. Mr Marriot! There is the matter of your provisional settlement. He looked at me over rimless spectacles. A uniform that five days ago had conveyed dapper servility now expressed paramilitary menace. His manner was utterly changed.

Your mask has slipped below your nose, Mr Marriot.

As I pulled out my wallet there was a sound of raised voices. I glanced over my shoulder. A strikingly handsome, bearded man in jeans and leather jacket, carrying a bunch of red roses, was trying to force his way through the revolving door. The older of the porters was blocking his path, arms outstretched. An elderly guest seemed to be trapped inside the door. The receptionist handed me a list of charges to check. And a petty irritation clicked in. I was told, I said, that whisky in the Cigar Lounge was on the house. The man consulted his screen. He clicked back and forth with his mouse, forehead wrinkled in diligent endeavour. Behind me the intruder was growing more and more agitated. Three uniforms converged. On the Tuesday, sir, the receptionist confirmed, but not on the Wednesday. I limped to the Breakfast Room.

At the door the young attendant took my temperature, twice. Then a third time. Sometimes it's erratic, sir. I explained that I had rushed down from the sixth floor, on the stairs, fearful that service would close. You will need to be quick, sir. He let me in.

There was no sign of Carmen. The room was freezing.

All the windows were open today. A dozen guests were winding up sombre meals. Only my old smoking companions, the Franco-Californian romance, had a bottle of wine on the table. At the buffet the staff were clearing up. I accepted cold cuts, roast potatoes and grilled veg, ordered a glass of Cabernet, and took three bread rolls and three packs of grissini.

Eating, I remembered how when things were bad with Connie I would go out and eat alone in expensive restaurants. It had been a pleasure then to focus entirely on the food. Now I worried that Carmen would suppose I didn't care about our appointment. Could I phone her? It would mean asking Reception to connect us. From my room, with my guests present. What I liked, I thought, about this woman was her blend of poise and poignancy. She wasn't unaware of her beauty, just focused on the predicament of the man she cared about. You are thinking again of what might have been with Rachel, I reflected. And why not? I said out loud. Miss West Coast glanced my way and smiled. They were getting up to go.

I raised my glass and smiled back. The roast potatoes were excellent. I opened the phone and scrolled through some headlines. *How the Virus Stole My Sense of Smell. NBA Suspends Season.* I lowered my nose to my plate and sniffed. All was well. *Chaos at Universities as Students Told to Stay Away.* Then, letting my mind wander back over the last few days, I realised that I wasn't in the end so unhappy with everything that was happening. Perhaps because I was no longer in the thick of life. I did not have to bring up a child, choose a country to live in, pursue a career, find a lawyer, deal with a violent partner, or nurse a sick one. On the contrary, missed appointments, damaged knees and unexpected guests all reminded me I was still alive. We are not now that strength which in old days . . . How did the line go? But that which we are, we are.

I watched the diners disperse. No doubt others were eating in their rooms. Afraid of infection. Or already infected. Was the Hotel Milano a hot spot, so called? Then it occurred to me I must cancel my trip to Ben's. Having been exposed. Email or phone call? Unexpectedly, I acknowledged a pang. I would miss seeing Sophie. It was a shame. Perhaps when we did meet again, I thought, I should finally try to talk to Ben. I pondered this. Talk about what exactly? Neither of us wanted to go over the past.

Back in my room, Hakim was anxious to hunt for the cat. Rania got to her feet and pulled up her mask as I came in. Omar was sleeping. I gave the boy a pack of grissini and asked what the doctor's verdict had been. I felt sleepy myself after the wine.

Rania swayed a little, arms folded.

Please, let's sit down.

We must look for Bibi, she said.

I realised she had showered while I was downstairs. The hair on her forehead was glossy. She said: If the fever will drop in the next day or so, he is okay.

If not?

She looked at me, dark eyes steady between mask and headscarf.

Rania – I used her name for the first time – your husband is not looking for a place for you, is he?

The boy came and tugged her arm.

We will go soon now, sir.

I'm not trying to throw you out. I'm trying to understand.

She put a hand on the boy's head, bent and whispered to him. Then met my eyes again: There is no need.

I took off my mask and put it on the desk. I hated wearing it. She was struggling to contain the boy. We will leave the hotel, she said, as soon as he can move.

I like you all, I told her. And I have the room till Saturday. You're welcome to stay.

The boy scowled at me, hanging on his mother's arm. She softened: Where will we look for Bibi? Do you think?

Who knows? Maybe he's gone back to the attic. I smiled. For some peace and quiet.

Bibi is a lady, she said, not a boy.

I went out on the balcony, leaving the windows open to change the air. The yellow balloon was still there. The entrance to the hotel was quiet. Likewise the big plaza. Not a siren. Not a plane in the sky. No one was entering or leaving the station. Curious, I thought, that the man they had chased away had been carrying red roses. Perhaps it was okay not to know what was really going on with my guests. On the other hand, imagine the police storming the room and arresting me for protecting criminals.

I leaned over the balustrade and lit a cigarette. It was becoming a habit again – the past creeping back – though the pleasure lay more in the business of opening the pack, touching the springy stubs, striking the match, than in

174

actually smoking. You still feel a desire to seduce these women, I realised. Rania, Carmen. You hanker for their trust. Such a sleaze, Connie would say.

I stubbed out the cigarette after a couple of puffs and went back into the room. Since Omar was lying to one side of the bed, I lay down on the other. Carmen would be around for dinner, I thought. So what's the difference? In the quiet afternoon his breathing was louder than ever. I turned on my side and studied his face. A foreign man. The skin pigment subtly different from anything I knew. His beard thickening. There was a heartening decency about him somehow, in the cut of the cheeks, the mouth and the chin. How does one get these impressions? I had enjoyed it when he spoke to the boy in Arabic. It sounded at once harsh and affectionate. What did I know? You are eager to seduce others and they seduce you, I thought.

But soon I would fall asleep. It was coming. Recalling the pleasure of pulling the blanket over my head in the attic, I slipped down under the quilt. In the dark there was an animal smell. I lay still, getting warm, breathing my own breath. It was odd how his breathing made me think of waves and water. His book too, about the waters of the Nile. I still couldn't work out what kind of book it was. Then he drew a deeper breath. It rushed a little further up the beach, receded more slowly, dragging pebbles. I reached a hand under the quilt and found his, clammy and rough. A starfish. Blessed are the waters. The words came from nothing. Blessed are the waters that wash over us. Now there was the old question of whether Connie and Rachel would ever meet. Will they, won't they? Two great phases of existence. We are walking barefoot on the sand. You are not ill, I tell Rachel. We embrace and over her shoulder I find eyes staring from the seaweed.

Please! Please, sir!

Rania was shaking my shoulder.

Listen!

His breathing was worse, his face strained with effort. I sat up on the edge of the bed. I felt shattered.

We must . . . pull him, she said. Up on the pillows. The doctor said.

Hakim stood by the television, biting his lip. There was no sign of the cat.

I went round his side of the bed. Rania knelt on the quilt. We piled up three pillows, gripped his armpits. His head fell back. The mouth opened. He was heavier than I expected. Or I was weaker. His fleece was soaking. Like- wise the quilt cover. As we settled him our eyes met.

Smells are good, I said.

She didn't get it. We must change sheets, she said.

Stepping back, my knee sent a sharp pain through thigh and hip. Falling asleep had been such a joy.

You must call Reception. Ask for new sheets.

I explained that only this morning I had told them I didn't want anything. I had turned away new towels.

Hakim came and stood beside his grandfather. He put a hand on his head and bent to whisper.

Tell them you are spilling something. On the bed.

They will be suspicious.

She shook her head. Guests ask crazy things. All the time.

And when they bring the sheets? You can't all hide on the balcony. It's cold out there.

She crossed the room, opened the French windows and came back, eyes frowning. I looked at Omar. His breathing was a little easier. But everything in the bed was damp. We'll have to change his clothes as well, I said.

I got up and went to the phone. I would be grateful if you could leave fresh sheets and towels outside my door. Room 607. I'm afraid I spilled some wine. I will put out the used sheets afterwards in the laundry bag. I don't want anyone taking risks on my behalf.

Sir, our staff have masks and gloves and sanitising products.

I prefer to do it myself.

There was silence.

I am seventy-six. I have a weak heart. Besides, I have nothing to do.

The sheets came with a discreet knock. Omar had sunk into a feverish sleep. There was no protest when we pulled off his jeans and underwear. We got his backside on a towel. Rania cleaned him with a flannel. I rolled him over while she wiped. Neither of us commented on this intimacy. Then there was the struggle to get his arms in the sleeves of my spare shirt. Fortunately we were about the same size. When we were done, I collapsed in an armchair while she washed his things in the bath. Hakim had started running again. His feet thumped back and forth. I noticed that as he ran he shouted silently. He crouched by the door, hands covering his face, muttering, sprang to his feet, ran like mad to the window, eyes wild, lips working, then crouched down again. Taking cover.

Rania carried the desk chair out onto the balcony to hang the clothes. Coming back in, she was crying. I hadn't expected this and wondered what would happen if Omar died. How do you explain a corpse in your bed? Now my phone rang. I fished it from my pocket. Once again it was the New York number. Was it Deborah? Or some polite young subeditor asking for a short piece on the funeral? I refused the call. Rania sat on the bed and turned away to lower her mask and blow her nose. When she turned back, she said, He is a good man. He is good to Hakim.

We had a good talk this morning, I said.

Her eyes narrowed. After a moment she asked: You really have a weak heart, sir?

No. And I'm not seventy-six either.

We looked at each other. I found it maddening that I couldn't see her nose and mouth. If you think he needs to go to hospital, I said, I'm sure we can find a way.

She shook her head. The doctor says hospital is the most dangerous place in this moment. She looked around, as if hoping to see something to do. Hakim dashed across the room.

Omar told me, I said, that he had bureaucratic troubles when he took his wife to hospital.

Rania turned away and put a hand on the man's forehead. We must give him water when he wakes up.

We were silent a while. No sign of the cat then? I asked.

She rolled her eyes again. With a hint of playfulness. I couldn't make her out at all.

Do you want me to go and look for him? Sorry, her.

She shook her head. When the boy raced by she held out her arms but he brushed her aside.

I got to my feet. Why don't you two watch some television together? I'll go out and get some air. Do you want me to buy food?

She looked about her rather vaguely and I realised that for all the air of calculation she had no plan. Or if there had been one, it had fallen through.

XIX

Moments later I saw the cat. It was peeping from behind the white sofa opposite the lift. Sleek and black. What a hero I would be, I thought, if I took it back to the boy. It shot off towards the stairs. I hobbled after. Every few steps the animal looked over its shoulder, checking I was following. Bibi! I tried to coax. It padded on. Swift and dainty. The quest cheered me up. If one is chasing something, let it be beautiful. And harmless.

On the fifth floor the man from Housekeeping didn't notice when the creature ran under his trolley. We exchanged nods from behind our masks. The silliness was exhilarating. More dreamlike than dreams. I leaned hard into Excalibur. The cat waited at a turn of the stairs, head cocked, whiskers spread. Bibi! It raised its tail tall and tripped down the next flight. Connie loved cats. You should admire their sublime selfishness, Frank. Rachel thought all pets unworthy surrogates for human love.

We were at the fourth. The creature was sitting behind a pot with a pining money tree. I caught the glint of its eyes through limp fronds. Was it playing? I couldn't believe how much I was enjoying myself. I haven't coughed all day, I realised. I'm strong as an ox.

Bibi! I approached slowly. Bibi! The animal was very still and attentive. I will only catch her if she wants to be caught, I thought. How could I make that happen? With just the big plant between us I tried to crouch. My knee wouldn't bend. I reached out a hand. The cat pushed its head forward gingerly, to sniff. I could feel the dampness of the nose on the fingertips. I waited, tensed for the grab. Or should I try to stroke? Bibi, I whispered. The animal turned and trotted off, insouciant, flashing a wisp of white on its little buttocks. Along the corridor this time.

I followed. It was no madder than a million other tasks. We were heading for the Cigar Lounge. I pushed hard on my stick. The glass doors were to my right. I glimpsed a newspaper. Whisky would be nice. But now the cat was trapped. The corridor ended in a high window. There was a blue velvet curtain gathered in a sash. A fire extinguisher. The animal turned, at bay. I shuffled forward, hand extended. The space was easily wide enough for her to dash around me. All the same, there would be a critical moment when I might shoot out a hand. If I got down on the floor, perhaps, and lay crosswise?

Bibi . . .

She sat patiently, beneath the window. Regal in her fur. I took another step. In a bound she was on the sill. The move had been so fast I wasn't entirely sure I had seen it. So much for getting down on the floor. Now she stood on all four paws in stark silhouette against the urban twilight behind. Coal black, with prism eyes.

I took the stick in both hands and waved it left and right like a wand. This caught her attention. I closed in, moving the stick in little circles, figures of eight. The cat was fascinated. I was surprised I had thought of this. As if the animal itself had prompted me. Exactly as I moved to snatch it, there was a sharp hiss, a commotion of fur and claws, and she leapt up the curtain, onto the fire extinguisher.

Fab-u-lous!

From behind came a burst of laughter. Miss West Coast and her man were at the door of the Cigar Lounge.

Hi there. She came forward. I didn't know the hotel allowed pets.

They were arm in arm, masked. The air filled with perfume. An 'andsome pussy, the Frenchman said. He chuckled.

Oh please! She dug an elbow in his ribs. For a moment we were all jolly. As if there was no health crisis.

Poor thing, she was saying now. The animal was still clutching the curtain. She's frightened. Can I? She stepped forward. I love cats.

Go ahead. I wondered how she knew it was a she. I'm too old for this, I said.

Oh no, my friend, it's not a question of age! It's a feeling.

I was astonished to be called my friend. She slipped off her pink mask and dangled it just beside and above the animal. It was strange how naked the face seemed, unmasked. How creamy the skin, luscious the lips. She made little whispering noises, twitched a snub nose. Bibi's jet black against the deep blue velvet of the curtain was gorgeous. The creature detached a paw and patted the mask. Ever so carefully. Eyes intent. The woman twined the mask's elastic around slim fingers so that the pink slip jerked a little to the left, a little to the right. Teasing. Inviting. The Frenchman and I exchanged glances. A woman of many talents! he breathed. She had her willowy back towards us, white fur jacket over tight yellow dress. Tinkling bracelets, she reached her free arm to run a fingertip along its flank. There, my lovely, she whispered. There, my darling. The animal slithered down the curtain onto the windowsill, still trying to pat the mask. The woman led her on. My gorgeous, gorgeous, furry black jewel. You are so lovely, aren't you? Can I pick you up, little darling? Will you let me?

A moment later the black fur was cradled against the white. She was tickling its ear now. Oh, she just wants a little love, don't you, treasure? Like the rest of us. Just a little love in this miserable boring pandemic. She kissed the cat between the ears, then cried, Oh my God, I don't have my mask on!

And the moral of the story, the Frenchman laughed – he had pulled out a pack of cigarettes – is: never snatch at a pussy!

They both giggled.

We cannot eat the cat, Rania observed.

How I got it back to the room, I'm not sure. I needed both hands at all times. The stick tucked under an arm. Without that support, I leaned a shoulder on the wall every couple of steps. Between the Bugattis and the Aston Martins. The animal was uneasy; my whispering did not have the same effect as the young woman's. Was Bibi susceptible to expensive perfume perhaps? Vaguely I wished it had been Carmen who'd found me trying to catch her, Carmen dangling her mask, whispering sweet nothings. In Italian. I used a knuckle to call the lift, praying it would be empty. With the ding of its arriving, the cat wriggled furiously. Muscle and bone seemed to be squirming out of the fur. I held on tight, thinking fairy tales where hero wrestles with beast that turns into prince or princess.

At the door my keycard was in my back pocket. The slightest loosening of grip and the animal was gone. I tried to knock with my foot, but the sound wasn't sharp. Rania, it's Frank. There was no sound from within. I kicked a little harder. The cat writhed and strained, magically strong. In the end I had to grab it by the scruff of the neck with my left hand while my right went for the key. The back legs thrashed wildly. Who would have thought there could be so much energy in the thing?

Rania! She had put on the chain.

The door opened and we were in. I banged it shut with my shoulders. Released to the floor, Bibi streaked under an armchair and Hakim was down on his hands and knees after her.

You must wash, Rania said.

My knuckles were streaming blood. I held my hand under the cold water and studied myself in the mirror. Why had I done that? What does any of this have to do with Frank Marriot? I wound toilet paper around the wound. Two deep gouges. When I went back into the room, Rania said, Hakim is hungry. We cannot eat the cat.

And Omar?

He was awake, but still feverish, his breathing unchanged.

Do you think you can eat anything?

He said something to her in a low voice.

A soup, Rania said. Lentils.

I sank in a chair. They had been watching a children's programme. A blue dinosaur was drinking a glass of milk.

I will try to get something, Rania said. She opened the wardrobe where her coat was hanging beside my black jacket. She seemed very purposeful.

I thought you were worried that if you went out you couldn't get back in.

She buttoned the coat over her dungarees. It depends, she said.

We can order food to the room. I can get him some hot soup.

First I will try to go to the shops.

The door closed behind her. I dissolved aspirin and vitamin C in mineral water and sat beside Omar while he drank. He needed to go to the bathroom, he said. He swung his legs over the edge of the bed and I draped a bathrobe on his shoulders and took an elbow. What if I were to follow her? I wondered. But it seemed wrong to leave the boy alone with him.

Thanks, Frank, Omar muttered when he was back on the bed.

Hakim was fooling with the cat. It was almost six. I flicked between CNN, the BBC, Fox. New restrictions. Spiralling death toll. It was a fanfare of catastrophe. With already a touch of liturgical tedium. Quarantine rules. Infection counts. You could see we would be watching these figures for weeks ahead. Computer models. Ventilators. Vaccines. Mask types. The vast armoury of control. But then what was the Round Table, I caught myself thinking, but an instrument of control? Now a woman in a white coat was discussing the finer points of hand washing. We are all feeling very anxious and insecure said a man on a cruise ship denied entry to Sydney harbour.

Clearing his throat, Omar asked, What do you think, Frank?

I'm amazed, I said. I never imagined they would stop the world for old men like me.

We listened to a woman who had watched her father die on Skype.

It's very bad, he said. I am not working for two weeks.

I asked him what he did.

A market stall. Fruit and vegetables. You, Frank?

I used to write, for magazines.

You have had a good life, Frank. He managed a smile. Haven't you?

I was taken aback. It doesn't always feel like that, I said. After a moment I asked, What is a good life, Omar, do you reckon?

He thought about it while a doctor explained that he wore a nappy under his PPE.

I don't know. But I feel, talking to you, you have had a good life.

I was baffled. How could I give that impression? And you?

He stared at the TV. CNN's world weather.

It was good until Farah died.

His wife presumably. I couldn't think of anything to say.

Khalil took it badly. He blames Italy. And me.

The sick man had started to shake his head, slowly and rhythmically. At the same time he really seemed to be focused on a snowstorm over Ohio. The pictures were spectacular. All at once there was a sharp knocking at the door.

Please! Quickly!

I moved as fast as my knee would allow. Rania pushed in, panting. She shut the door herself, taking care not to slam. Then moved swiftly to the television. She stooped and pulled out the plug. Put a finger over her lips. Hakim! Shush. She was listening, chest lifting and falling. We all watched her. Were there footsteps in the corridor? We waited. At last she relaxed, hung her coat in the wardrobe and went to hug her son. The boy whispered excitedly.

Someone was following you, I said.

The two were on the floor stroking the cat.

A hotel man. She exchanged a glance with Omar.

You didn't get to the shops?

No.

I called Housekeeping to order a meal. The voice explained that a reduced menu was accessible on the television. Rania crouched to put the plug back in. I realised I was getting used to being around her: the quick thoughtfulness of her movements, a wary urgency about the eyes. We studied what was on offer. As much as one person could reasonably eat, I suggested. A carrot soup for Omar. Paccheri alla Vittorio for Hakim. A plate of roast beef for Rania. A side salad with mozzarella for myself.

Wine?

We don't drink alcohol.

I ordered a bottle of San Pellegrino. Please leave the tray at the door and knock.

And so we had a family evening. We watched a Pixar film. In Italian. Hakim sat on the floor, his back to the bed. Rania assisted Omar with the soup, finished it herself. His fever was rising again. She took a piece of meat to the balcony and shut the cat out there, then sat on the floor, gathering the boy between her legs. I was in the armchair, half watching the idiocies of the film, half their faces. She was still masked; he twisted his neck to chatter to her. Once she pulled down the mask to kiss his temple. Then we realised Omar was asleep. It had been a long day. And I had missed Carmen again. I opened the minibar. There were still two whiskies. Vodka, rum. A box of Scottish shortbread. A Diet Coke. I sipped Black Label from a tiny bottle. Hakim and Rania drank the Coke. The shortbread went around. One more day and I am out of here.

I woke to the sound of retching. Rania was cleaning vomit. Omar was leaning over the edge of the bed. The smell was strong.

Can I help?

Towels. One with cold water.

Approaching in the lamplight I realised she had neither headscarf nor mask. Her hair fell straight and girlish. The top button of her shirt was undone. I found the towels. One for the floor, the damp one for his forehead. Her wound was worse than I had thought. A jagged cut low in the cheek and a dark contusion at the corner of the mouth. Her lips pursed in concentration. Omar was shivering, muttering apologies. I wiped his face while she finished with the floor. Then she remembered her mask. Please, I said. I've seen. I can't unsee.

I retired to my armchair, coat over my shoulders. But Omar was restless. His fever high again. Rania moved Hakim to the edge of the bed. The boy was sleeping soundly. She sat on her heels between them, speaking in the cooing voice I had heard in the attic. His breath rasped. I couldn't work out if he was talking in his sleep, or consciously to her. Whether she was simply cooing to soothe him or conversing. I remembered Miss West Coast coaxing the cat with her soft voice. But now the night had well and truly begun. The moment when you are on your own. I drifted in and out of dreams. A mountain road narrower and narrower, until it was surely impossible our car could pass. Rania whispering, persuading. We should call an ambulance, I said. Awake again, I remembered the same words in Delhi. Rachel clammy and burning. No. I need fresh air. Take me to the mountains, Frank. I won't go to hospital. I tried to soothe her, speaking softly in the dark. The doctors hate me, Frank. They are killing me. I was confused. I wanted my woman to be brave, face the truth, so my admiration could remain intact. But it wasn't me dying. You're planning to leave me, she said. Do you have another woman already? She couldn't be still. I wanted to sink away in sleep, to bury myself in sleep. Only to wake when it was over. I should never have trusted you, Frank. Do something! For God's sake! I called Reception. How can we get to the mountains? No, now. Tonight. An hour later we were wrapped in blankets in the back of an Ambassador behind a turbaned driver. We will have a lovely holiday, Frank, won't we? She was lying across my lap. Yes, I said, of course. We'll take long walks. We will, yes. Climb the peaks? Yes. Together? Of course. And no more illness, Frank? Promise me, no more pain. I promise, I said. I swear to God.

Please?

Yes.

We must change his shirt.

I struggled to my feet. Again we raised him on the pillows. Peeled my smart shirt off his long arms. Again Rania sponged him down. He was shaking. We dressed him in the shirt that had dried in the afternoon. Almost dried. Then she lay down beside him and I rested, sitting on a corner of the bed. My hand felt sore from the cat's scratches. What devotion, I thought, to the father of the husband who had beaten her. She closed her eyes and the face smoothed. The neck was strong and young in the shadows. Probably younger than I had first thought. Mid twenties? It occurred to me it might be unusual for a woman from her world to have just one five-year-old child. Not to have gone at once for a second. For a while I speculated about their lives, watching the three of them in the low light from the French windows on the sixth floor of a silent hotel in a silent city. I thought how their story might be reported on the news feeds. To support this or that agenda. Without any of us knowing what that story really was. Omar had settled now. And he too seemed younger. Late fifties? In his prime really. Big choices still to be made. He began to snore. I reached out a hand and laid it on his forehead. It was cool. The fever was gone. Was it? My heart lifted.

There was no question of sleep. I put on my coat and went out on the balcony, pulling the French windows closed behind me. The cat was curled in a corner. Rania had given her a cushion. I leaned on the balustrade and lit a Winston Churchill. Puffed it alight. You have had a good life, Frank. Why on earth had he said that? I felt weirdly happy. Then I noticed a turd, in a corner. Perhaps I could scrape some earth, I thought, from the plant pots round the hotel.

Enjoying the swagger of the cigar, I leaned out into the night. And I thought how easy it would be to throw oneself off this balcony. Now. To plunge down through the branches, onto the pavement. Maybe liberating that yellow balloon *en passant*. Or onto a taxi. Drive me to the mountains, *Signore*. It has always seemed possible I might kill myself on impulse one day. Were the circumstances right. I imagined an email to Deborah. I will not be applying for the editorship, Deborah. I no longer believe that journalism . . .

Enough. I looked at the cat. You don't bother with this kind of stuff, do you, Bibi? The animal was fast asleep.

Giddy from the smoke, I went inside and sat at the desk. I have spent so much of my life at desks. Without thinking, I opened my banking app and moved eighty thousand pounds to Ben's account. Journalism has become a curse, I thought. One learned more about the world from chasing a cat. Changing a sick man's sheets. Suddenly it occurred to me that I had been lucky to go through all that agony with Rachel. That was a mad thought. I sat up and stared at the imitation Kirchner. It was ironic that although twisted together the man and woman were looking away from each other. Dear Connie, I started an email, picking at the glowing screen in the dark, my hand still smarting from the scratches. F-o-r . . . Forget, the phone prompted. Forgive, I wrote, my s . . . sins, Android guessed. I smiled; slowness. Thanks for explaining about (b-e . . . being) Ben. One thing: since Dan's (f-u . . . function) funeral, I've been (t . . . trying) thinking how (l . . . long) lucky we (t . . . truly) three were to know each other. What a (f-i . . . fickle) fine time it was. And how (s . . . special) smart of us not to (e-n . . . enjoy) end up (k-i . . . kissing) killing each other. There were times when it felt like a (c-l . . . classic) close-run thing. Anyway, the (p . . . problem) past is (a-l . . . almost) always (p-r-e . . . preventing) present, which is why (l . . . love) life sometimes feels like a (d . . . day) dream. Look after yourself. Frank.

Could I send a message like that? Did it make sense to push my stick so deep into the old slime? It was 4.30 a.m. I sent it.

I went to the bathroom, shut the door, ran a bath. Why was I feeling so odd? You are yearning, I realised, to declare your love to someone. How dangerous was that? But it had been brewing since the start of this trip. Lancelot mused a little space; / He said, She has a lovely face.

192

And I had gone straight to the cash desk. There is a sort of surplus, in me, I sensed. Of energy. Perhaps the same that fed my famous frankness. I have to declare myself to someone. To Carmen, Miss West Coast, Rania. Or to Omar, to Hakim, the cat. Some emotion that had to out. Do something rash, Frank, something humbling and joyous. Why? Because I had no partner? I needed a pet? Or was I experiencing some kind of spiritual awakening? Having sat in the chair where you lose yourself to find yourself. I slipped down into the deep tub until the water covered my face. It was deliciously warm. You are seventy-five, I thought. Muddled, submerged, undefined. Yet happy. Omar would survive. And Saturday I would be home. All is well.

XX

In the corridor a young man was trotting back and forth in shorts and running shoes. Between the fifth and fourth floors an oriental woman was using the stairs to stretch. With dumbbells in her hands. The Grand Hotel Milano had become a five-star hamster wheel. Both exercisers wore masks, in the big empty spaces. The stairs were painful. It was six thirty. Day was dawning. And it occurred to me that if I took the lift down to the basement, bypassing the ground, very likely there wouldn't be anyone to make trouble for me.

So it was. A simple ruse. In the basement there was a smell of fresh bread. A sound of voices and a clatter. I passed the gym and spa, saw a trolley being drawn into another lift. The service lift. At the end of a zigzag of corridors the depot was busy. Men in orange vests were wheeling bins out onto the pavement. A lorry throbbed in the street. I made myself unobtrusive and hobbled past, wondering again who that coffin had been for. How many people in the hotel were ill?

The streets too were an exercise park. For people and dogs. They served no other purpose. I counted five runners

194

in as many minutes. All but one masked. I leaned on my stick and lit a cigarette. You cannot wear a mask when you smoke and for some reason smoking was permitted. I would give up, I told myself, when I reached the airport for the flight home.

There were no police about. No ambulances even. Outside a well-appointed apartment block two elderly women rummaged in a line of bins. Again I wondered what exactly had prompted my guests to move into the hotel attic. Where would they go when I left?

The morning was mild, overcast, damp. At the super-market I checked the opening times. Today was Friday. 13 March. I smiled. 7.30. I lurched down the street, past shuttered cafes. To kill half an hour I would do a round of the block, admire a palazzo or two. A tram squealed, completely empty, the driver masked. Never had it occurred to me how important faces are in making a place. But then who would have thought they could be taken away? On the plus side, there was birdsong. The pavements were lined with tall plane trees. A blackbird flung its bright tune into the teeth of the general melancholy. I listened and whistled back. People crumbled to dust for Percivale, I thought, because he couldn't see them for worrying about the grail. The blackbird flew to a higher branch and trilled. It seemed important that its beak was yellow.

When I returned to the room, Omar was sitting up. The boy was out on the balcony. Rania was in the bathroom. I spread my purchases on the desk.

I have taken a shower. Omar was smiling.

195

You're feeling better.

He moved his head from side to side in an odd, expressive gesture. Chest tight, he said. He bumped a fist on his sternum.

Take it easy.

I had brought them takeaway coffee. Croissants. Sandwiches. And I've found you a phone, I told Rania. She came out of the bathroom in a robe, a towel gathering her hair. None of us wore masks. She examined the box and shot me a perplexed look.

It was the only model they had. At the supermarket. I hope it takes your SIM.

We must pay you back, Frank, Omar said. There was still a rasp in his breath. Hakim ran in from the balcony and pounced on the food. Sitting down, I found myself noticing Rania's bare feet. Her toenails were a shiny blue.

Soave sia il vento, I hummed to myself, heading for the Breakfast Room. Life was good, I thought. Carmen greeted me warmly when I sat at her table. No mention was made of my absence at lunch or dinner.

What time? I asked. The operation.

Ten. She looked at her watch. It was 9.15.

I . . . She looked for words, plucking apart a croissant. I cannot visit him. Forbidden.

I shook my head. When will you know? News of the operation?

She swallowed. In the afternoon. And she licked a fingertip.

I laughed. Nice jam!

Yes. For a moment there was the sly smile I had seen once before. Luxury *marmellata*!

Omar was smiling too. Rania had brought down the suitcase from the attic. Hakim had recovered his toys. The crisis was over, life restarting, the show on the road. Tomorrow they would be ready to leave the hotel. Rania had the new phone on charge and was already making calls, crouched at the socket behind an armchair.

Where will you go?

Omar had his eyes closed.

Perhaps Bari. My sons.

I thought travel was forbidden.

Everything is forbidden, he said.

Hakim had the television on. Nothing is as inexhaustible as the supply of children's cartoons. Rania brought the phone to Omar to make a call. I picked up Tennyson and decided to leave them to it. It was my last day in Milan. There would be much to mull over in the months to come. I sat on the white sofa by the lift and read poems at random. Can calm despair and wild unrest / Be tenants of a single breast? No prizes for answering that one. When was age so crammed with menace? madness? written, spoken lies? Indeed.

Now there was a text message from Alitalia. Important changes to your upcoming flight. It had been moved forward from 6 p.m. Saturday 14 March to 8 a.m. I could accept this or switch to a flight at 8 a.m. on Sunday 15 March. I read the message carefully a second time to make sure I had understood. Would my guests, I wondered, be ready to get out of the room so early? And this reminded me of the phone calls from the American number, yesterday. Deborah was passing through Saturday morning. Could I see her, having been exposed, presumably, to this illness? But then, should I really have seen Carmen at breakfast? Why hadn't I thought of that? No, I *had* thought of it. Then unthought it, as it were. I had kept my distance. All the same. I decided to phone the number. Just as the voicemail clicked on I realised that if the phone was really in the States it would be five o'clock in the morning there. Hi, said a familiar voice, Connie is not available right now. Please leave your message after the tone.

The beep came. I took a deep breath and closed the call. It really was her voice. Of old. And back in the USA. Perhaps she had been there for years. What did I know? It was a rule with Ben that we never speak of his mother. The last thing I need is to hear my parents badmouthing each other. Dear Ben – I started an email – I realise I will have to cancel my visit Sunday since I'm supposed to quarantine after the trip to Italy. Please tell Sophie I will bring her presents as soon as I can. I'll phone on the day!

I sent the email. So it was Connie who had been calling me. How strange. You came to Dan's funeral on the off chance of seeing Connie. And you wrote that strange note to her last night. Something had shifted. So let's speak, I decided. Let's open a new phase. Dear Deborah, I wrote, I'm worried about our meeting tomorrow morning since I fear I may have been exposed to the virus. What do you think? I clicked the link in the Alitalia email and opted for the Sunday-morning flight. I would wear two masks and rubber gloves, but I was going to fly.

Not a soul was to be seen. From the white sofa on the sixth-floor landing. Not a person passed by. The air was uncannily still. Like being in a pyramid, I thought, as the ages unfold, the ages when Egypt was envied for its waters and dead pharaohs were tucked away in secret chambers with an assortment of knick-knacks to get them through eternity. I remembered Dan's prayer cap. Did they put swords in the tombs too? I turned again to The Passing of Arthur and again found the passage where the dying king sends Sir Bedivere to toss Excalibur in the lake. But the good knight disobeys. The sword is too valuable, too dense with history. Arthur is furious. Bedivere tries a second time but he can't let go. He hides the sword in the reeds. So, a mortally wounded man trusts a loyal friend to throw away the thing most precious to him. That most represents him. To send it back whence it came. Whence we all came. Out of the slime. He wants the story to end. Now he's ready to kill Bedivere for his betrayal. The knight goes a third time. The magical third. Shuts his eyes and throws. The great brand made lightnings in the splendour of the moon. I gripped my stick hard. Why did I find this so moving? But ere he dipt the surface, rose an arm / Clothed in white samite, mystic, wonderful / And caught him by the hilt, and brandished him three times, and drew him under in the mere.

It was nonsense, beautiful nonsense. All the same, I had done the right thing to choose the Tennyson, I decided. Given the nature of this trip. Though Montaigne no doubt was the plainer speaker. And in general, I thought, breathing deeply on the white sofa on the sixth floor of the Hotel Milano, in general I had done the right thing in the various crises of my life. The right thing leaving Connie, and Dan. The right thing writing Power of Good. The end of my professional life. The right thing cremating Rachel in Shimla.

I'm sorry, sir. Let me try again.

But the polite young man had already tried twice. Since the Chinese contingent were right behind me I stood aside to let them through. And again I explained that I had hurried down the stairs from the sixth and this must have got me sweating. The Chinese all wore rubber gloves and were scrupulous about their masks and distances.

I'm afraid you have 37.9, sir. You could try to rest for a few minutes and come back when you are cooler. Or you can order food in your room.

Turning away, I was face-to-face with Carmen. She raised an eyebrow.

I'm too hot, I said. I pulled a face, frustrated by the mask.

Her eyes showed concern.

I'll come back. In a few minutes. News?

She shook her head.

There were toilets at the back of the lobby beyond the lifts. I plunged my hands in a basin of cool water, rinsed cheeks and forehead, doused my bald pate, and shivered. The mirror was crystal clear, yet my face seemed to be breaking up. Patterned ripples of age, sinking jowls, weedy tufts of eyebrow. I stared, fascinated, dismayed. Then it all

200

pulled together in a smile. Still here, I thought. Ready to dive straight back in. All the same I decided not to go back to the Breakfast Room.

Riding the lift to the sixth, I wondered whether it had been a mistake switching my flight to Sunday. What time would Connie see I had phoned and, presumably, phone back? Should I tell her where I was? Knowing that she would pass that on to Ben who would then be upset that I had pretended to be home. Though I had never actually said as much. I touched my keycard to the lock and found the privacy chain was on.

Rania?

There was no response.

Rania, it's Frank.

The room was quiet.

Hakim! Omar!

Came a sound of swift footsteps and the door slammed shut. Now I heard a shout. Rania's voice. And another voice shouting over hers. A new voice. Then Hakim's shrill squeal.

I stared at the door. Surely they would open again in a moment or two. The quarrel went on. The new voice was sharp and urgent. Omar joined in. Then a cry. Rania? Hakim? I must go down to Reception. Perhaps. Or phone down. But how to explain? Something crashed. A hush. Then a wild repeated yell. I touched keycard to lock, turned the handle quietly, placed the rubber tip of my stick against the thin chain and gave an almighty shove. There was a splintering sound, the stick lunged forward; I was in.

At once I was confronted by a tall, bearded man, in

leather jacket and jeans. The floor was scattered with red roses and broken glass. He was blocking the passage to the room proper. A powerful man. I couldn't see the others. He spoke sharply, waved a hand. I remember veins in the forearm. Perhaps he was telling me to get out. When he came forward, I pressed back against the door. Omar was speaking behind. He reached for the handle beside me. I felt his breath on my face. No! I pressed hard against the door. Our eyes met. He turned and rushed back into the room.

I hobbled after him. Rania was crouched beside the bed, hugging Hakim who had his face hidden in her blouse. Omar was dressed, on his feet. He had shaved and looked pale, leaning against the wardrobe beside his daughter-in-law.

What's going on?

The man turned to me and spoke abruptly.

Khalil.

He stopped.

We spoke on the phone. I was struggling to sound calm. Remember? He didn't understand. You were in the hotel lobby yesterday.

Omar started speaking, perhaps translating.

Nice roses, I said. Perhaps I smiled. Khalil took a quick step towards me and raised a hand. Gleaming with rings. I managed not to move.

Omar tugged his jacket. The big man hesitated. When he dropped his hand, Omar said: He wants to take Rania and Hakim to the airport. He has tickets.

Why don't we talk about it?

I sounded feeble, sardonic. Khalil pushed his father

away and went to stand over Rania and the boy. Hakim was peeping through his fingers. Rania was defiant. Unmasked, unscarfed. They all started to speak. A crescendo of Arabic. Dangerously intense. Behind his anger, Khalil seemed baffled. He could not understand her resistance. He reached down and grabbed the boy's arm. Rania clung to the boy. The phone rang.

It was the hotel phone. I lurched towards it, but Khalil was wonderfully fast. Whirling round, his fist came down on the receiver. He held it down. Again we were face-to-face. His eyes were angry, but pleading too. Glancing down I could see thick hair on his knuckles.

Omar began to speak. He had slumped down on the bed. His voice was wheedling. He had no authority. The son wouldn't listen. The struggle was between husband and wife. As soon as the phone stopped ringing Khalil went back to her. She had the boy in her arms again. He spoke more calmly, gently even. Dropping to his knees, he picked up a rose and offered it to her. She turned away. His voice hardened. The boy clung to her. Khalil was speaking very fast. Whatever it was he said caused Omar to cry out. Now Khalil was reaching for his son's arm. With lightning decision he grabbed the boy and wrenched him from his mother's arms. She scrambled to her feet. Hakim wailed. His father dragged him towards the door. When Rania lunged Khalil struck her across the face with the back of a hand. I took three steps and fired by an excruciating pain in the knee raised Excalibur and whacked him with all the strength I had on the side of the head.

XXI

Now it's my turn. The fever has come. The dry cough. The tightness in the chest. Now I am the sick one. Confined to my room. Fatigued, listless. The phone rang again. After the fight. The call came through waves of pain. How had I ended up on the bed? For a moment I thought, my phone, and I thought, Connie. It wasn't in my pocket. And it wasn't my ringtone. I struggled to my elbows. The ringing stopped.

Some time later there was a knock at the door. I was awake enough now to be anxious that no one see the state the room was in. But a stone slab lay on my chest. I might eventually get to my feet, but never quickly enough to stop someone with a passepartout from coming in.

A voice called, Sir!

Yes? I coughed.

Communication for you, sir.

Put it under the door. My voice sounded strained.

I lay still a little longer, eyes closed, exploring discomfort. Had someone lifted me onto the bed, I wondered, or had I climbed up here myself? The quilt smelt of Omar. You still have your sense of smell, I noticed. Now there was a strange wailing. A seagull's cry perhaps. Am I imagining this? I opened my eyes and studied the ceiling. The cry came again. Struggling onto my side, I found glowing eyes at the window, wiry whiskers.

Dear sir or madam . . .

Consequent, it seemed, on my registering a corporeal temperature above 37.5° Celsius on three separate occasions government regulations obliged me to remain in my room. For fourteen days. Under no circumstances was I to move around the hotel. Food would be brought to my room as requested. Any requirements should be communicated to Housekeeping.

A letter addressed to me personally reminded me that I was checking out of the hotel tomorrow, Saturday 14 March, before midday. There seemed to be no communication between these two missives.

In any event, the room was a mess. Picking up the pieces, I tried to recall what had happened. There were twenty red roses in all. Khalil must have hoped the gift would reawaken love. The broken glass seemed to be one of the room's two tumblers. There was a mark on the wall where the plaster was broken. Who had thrown it? I put some roses in the other tumbler with a little water, and propped the long stems against the wall. Then two more in the slim tulip vase. Bibi mewed and pawed.

I rested a while on the armchair, headache coming and going. And noticed my phone. It was against the wall by the bedside table. But first the broken glass. I made an effort to study the floor. Take one thing at a time. At least I seemed able to focus. Instead in those last frantic minutes with my guests I had lost my presence of mind. I had cracked Khalil on the head. He staggered, then turned on me. Everyone yelling. The stick torn from my hand. A flurry of blows. Then my own head crashing back. I took Luxury Shopping in Milan from the desk and used it to sweep the fragments into a heap. The last thing a cat needs is glass in its paws. Slipping a page underneath, I scooped the lot into the waste bin.

What next? I remembered Omar beside me. For a moment I had had the impression his body was over mine, protecting mine. Or trying to. I had no clear picture of events. A door had slammed. More shouting. Omar was gone and then there was thumping. Not the footsteps in the attic. Someone banging on the bathroom door.

I should take a look at the phone. What time was it? And let the cat in. I was coughing again. There is a certain pleasure in savouring pains, if they're receding. Connie had been my undoing. Vaguely, I understood that Rania had got Hakim into the bathroom. They were locked in there. Khalil was beside himself. Perhaps the flight was leaving soon. I remember I had been contemplating their black suitcase, a few inches from my head, all zipped up and ready to go, when the phone rang. Mine this time. Automatically, I pulled it from my pocket. The American number. Connie. What bizarre circumstances in which to renew our relationship. But at once Khalil was upon me. I tried to curl into a ball. The phone was gone.

Bibi!

Now that I had opened the window, the cat was circumspect. Tail erect, she sniffed the space a while, then

206

shot into the room, looking for food. Eventually, she came to brush against an ankle.

Had Rania and Khalil, I wondered, made a deal, left together? Or had she hung on in the bathroom till Omar told her the coast was clear? Who had helped me onto the bed? Was it criminal of them to have abandoned me like that, or had I muttered that I was okay?

Now it occurred to me to check my wallet and passport. Where had I left them? In my inside pocket. Cards and cash were all there. And my trusty stick by the television. Good. There was a pack of grissini on the desk. I crumbled a couple into the fruit bowl and set it on the floor. Doing so, I noticed another rose under the armchair. I fished it out. Rania must have flung them across the room. I held its crimson to my nose and in an instant travelled back twenty years. I had bought red roses for Connie's birthday. Perhaps twenty, even thirty. An extravagant number. Extravagantly expensive. Connie's birthday is in January. It was a winter of discontent. Ben was on the sofa with his girlfriend when I came in with this explosion of colour. The two were impressed. They wanted to open a bottle. Connie wiped her hands on a dishtowel, took the roses, opened the trash and crushed them in there. You're cheating on me, she said. You've been cheating on me for years, I answered. So why the flowers? she asked.

It was a good question. I sat down and held the rose to my nose. Why does a man buy flowers for a woman he is fighting with? I remembered the pleading look in Khalil's eyes when he put his hand on the phone. One acts one way, as if something were over, yet goes on believing it might

207

still work out. Was that it? Perhaps I had cared so much about plain speech because I found it so difficult to speak plainly myself. Never buy flowers for me again, Connie said. Okay?

I never bought flowers for Rachel. We bought them together. To brighten a room or table. Every time we arrived in a new place. A rose is more beautiful when there is nothing riding on it. You see more clearly how the petals enfold light and dark. I slid the flower into the tumbler with the others. Parting gift from my guests, I thought.

But my phone was dead.

The cat leapt up beside me on the bed. She wasn't concerned that I was coughing. She patted the quilt and picked her spot. Hakim will miss you, I murmured. Were they at the airport now? Or had they split up? How different the week would have been if I had simply complained that there was a thumping noise in the room above.

The fever came and went. Eventually, I found the energy to go to the bathroom and wash the new wound on my head. Ugly, but not serious. I took two aspirin. The scratches on my hand were more painful. Someone's in the wars! I addressed my reflection; he raised an eyebrow and coughed. A wounded knight, I thought, must be nursed to health by queen or princess. In the early days with Rachel I had imagined her ministering to me at the end. It had seemed feasible.

Well, Bibi?

The cat opened half an eye.

I rang Housekeeping and ordered food. A glass of milk. Pasta. A piece of chicken. My flight has been delayed till

Sunday morning, I told Reception. I'll need a wake-up call at five thirty and a taxi to the airport. Yes, sir, said the voice.

Meantime evening had fallen. I turned on the TV and turned it off again. An orgasm of alarm. I was too tired for opera. Or even a film. I found my reading glasses and opened Tennyson at random. Dear is the memory of our wedded lives, / And dear the last embraces of our wives. Closed it. What would Connie make of my phone being off? Should I try to get hold of another somehow? I imagined a boat adrift in the ocean, no direction save the passing hours.

The food arrived. I felt shivery, but managed half the pasta. Bibi was ruthless with the chicken. I put her plate on the desk beside mine and watched her nudge the pale meat with her nose, lick it lovingly, then tear at it with vicious teeth. I remembered this morning's blackbird, chirping so blithely in the deserted street.

More aspirin, more reverie. In bed my breathing seemed normal enough. A slight snarl in the current perhaps. At the top of the lungs. All you can do in the end is close your eyes and wait. But now I was brought back to life by a strange grating sound. Bibi was on an armchair, dragging her claws across its dark blue leather. I threw the Tennyson at her and she jumped off and scampered round the room. She patted at a black cloth crumpled against the wall. Had Rania left a scarf? The cat rolled herself inside it, leapt away, pounced back. Had Rania been negotiating with her husband throughout? I wondered. Was that why she disappeared sometimes? I got up and opened the French windows a little so Bibi could come and go.

And suddenly remembered my refusal to apologise. That had been the defining moment. Yes. Not the article as such, but my refusal to apologise. Occasion too of the last phone call with Dan, the last direct communication from Connie. Give 'em a few words, Frank, to the effect that you didn't mean to offend, you weren't implying deliberate malice. That will do it. Don't be so proud, Connie wrote. Sackcloth's in fashion! I don't want my son's father to be a pariah. But I did mean to offend, Dan. I did imply malice. And I am proud, Connie. Proud to be a pariah.

Why on earth was I thinking of this now? Something on the TV? A celebrity apologising for having said she felt humiliated by the sanitary restrictions. She grovelled. Her words had been misunderstood. You're well out of this, Bibi, I muttered. The cat purred, and I was struck by the thought that the animal must have seen whether Khalil and Rania had left together, yet there was no way you could get this information from her. Should I call the police?

The pillow was too hot. I turned it over. Connie would suppose I had chickened out of the call. She had been heartened by my email. Or appalled. Never doubt, she wanted to tell me, that you are Ben's father. Or, I have to confess, Frank, when I fell pregnant . . .

Bibi purred. Our heads were inches apart. Sleep, she was telling me. Sleep.

My boat drifted onward through the evening and the night. In the bathroom I noticed a hairgrip. Towards dawn the French windows slammed. Soaked in sweat, I changed my shirt and somehow found the energy to wash out the soiled one. I put on my coat and took the shirt out on the balcony to dry. The wind was gusting. I felt faint but stirred, in the open air above the empty plaza, facing the great facade of the station. Departures, I thought, and I thought no one would notice if I used the Luxury Shopping guide to push the cat shit between the stone pillars and down into the street. In bed again, it occurred to me this wind might free that balloon. It would sail off into the sky. At some point I must check.

This fitful journeying was torpedoed the following morning by the sharp trill of the hotel phone. Bright daylight was in the room. I imagined lodging a complaint that there was no extension by the bed. It seemed odd in a luxury hotel. But the ringing persisted.

Sir, I have a call from Signora Rizzi.

Thank you. I waited, suddenly wide awake. Carmen, good morning.

At the other end of the line, silence.

Carmen?

There was a deep sigh. Please. Excuse me.

Carmen!

Can we meet?

I hesitated, trying to think. I'm afraid I'm ill. I'm sorry. I spoke slowly and clearly. I have a fever.

Ah. Okay.

I would be happy to see you. But I don't want to infect you.

Excuse me. Okay. Her voice trembled.

I'm thinking of Alberto. If you . . .

She began to sob.

Carmen.

She had put the phone down.

Between fits of coughing I ordered orange juice, coffee and croissants. And I asked Reception if they could call Signora Rizzi for me.

That line is busy, sir.

Could you keep trying?

It's Saturday morning, I realised. Tomorrow I would have to be up at the crack of dawn for my flight. But now the cat had found something to play with on the floor. She was patting it back and forth. Something small and shiny. She frisked this way and that, till her prey was trapped in the corner. I went to look, lowering myself down against the wall as I had in the attic. It was a ring. For a finger much slimmer than mine. Silver by the looks, but fashioned for half of the circumference as though it were arabic script.

The phone rang and I struggled to my feet.

Yes?

Excuse me, she said again.

Carmen, it's no problem.

What is . . . the number? Your room.

Ah. Six zero seven. But are you sure?

There was a brief silence.

I am ill, I repeated. We wouldn't want –

My father is in coma, she said. I cannot see him.

There was a knock at the door. Your breakfast, sir.

I covered the receiver. Thank you!

Carmen was trying to speak, but emotion had the better of her. She swallowed. Six zero seven?

Yes.

Somehow I got the tray into the room. How could I have read the situation so wrong? Hadn't I said your husband at some point? I thought I had. And she hadn't corrected me.

I poured milk for Bibi, then sat at the desk with coffee and croissant. Something felt strange. I was shivery. I must put on my trousers if she was coming. Rachel and I were always being mistaken for daughter and father. Once when she objected to the price of a concert ticket, the woman at the desk said, What do you care, dear, when Daddy's paying?

Returning to my food, I realised the strange thing was it had no smell. What a fool I'd been. I put my nose right inside the croissant. For weeks afterwards, Rachel called me Sugar Daddy and I would mutter, Spoiled Brat. We found it hilarious.

I ate quickly, but Carmen didn't come. Bibi was pawing at the window. She needed to get out. When I turned the handle, the wind burst in. A gale was blowing. I struggled to get the door shut.

Resting in the armchair, I had the impression my ears were singing. And noticed the imitation Kirchner again. How my world had shrunk. A couple of chairs, coffee table, bed, padded wardrobes, polished marble floor. And this odd painting of two bodies twisted together. Alberto, I thought, had flown north from Sicily with his daughter. To face an operation. He seemed a pleasant, accomplished man. I remembered how his eyes had followed her to the breakfast buffet.

For a while I wasn't sure whether I was thinking or

dreaming. I wandered through an untidy house looking for space to sit and work, stretched a plastic sheet over a mattress in a dusty room, fiddled with a bicycle chain. It was Ben's bike, I thought. Suddenly two sounds had me sitting up. Bibi crying to come back in. And a soft knock at the door.

I had a fresh mask ready. She was wearing a long skirt and blue cardigan. Her eyes were bloodshot, but her hair freshly washed. At once she saw the face at the window.

My cat. Bibi.

Inside, the animal made straight for the bed. Carmen seemed puzzled. She had her phone in her hand. I have the translation app, she tried to smile. I pointed to the arm-chair. Sitting, she leaned back, hands wide on the leather arms. Then closed her eyes. Thank you, she said.

For heaven's sake.

I coughed into my mask. I felt sad for her and happy for myself. After a few moments I said, The operation went badly?

Still with her eyes closed, she dipped and lifted her chin.

A person can recover from a coma.

This time she moved her chin from side to side.

His brain . . . it does not . . .

She opened her eyes and made to consult her phone. Respond?

She nodded. I cannot go to him. I cannot be with him.

She pulled off the mask and tossed it on the floor, muttered something sharp in Italian. I sat still. I could hardly move to comfort her. Exposed, her face was compelling.

As if I hadn't seen anything else all week. Lips swollen, chin quivering.

What will you do? I asked.

She opened her eyes wide and looked up.

Wait?

Her phone rang. She checked the screen, jumped to her feet and, speaking very rapidly, began to walk to the door.

Carmen! I felt in my pocket for the keycard. You have it.

XXII

I took to my bed. Oddly, I recalled the burning hoop at the top of endless stairs. Reading was beyond me now. Turning on my side I became aware of my heart. Thumping. There had been an awful lot of thumping these last few days. Don't be anxious, Frank, a voice warned.

I closed my eyes and let the day unfold. My last in the Grand Hotel Milano. If I slept now I should be in better shape when the wake-up call came tomorrow morning. It would be good to be back in my own flat, my own bed.

Wind pressured the window. I heard raindrops too. My hearing seemed very acute. Heartbeat and raindrop. Was a news story on CNN any more real than shadowy figures climbing stairs to pass through a hoop? In a dream. Or a voice that says: You are at their disposal?

I heard the cat padding here and there. It seemed uncannily loud. Puss in boots. An 'andsome pussy! I remembered Miss California dangling her pink mask. Everyone is always present, perhaps, if you let them. Then I was trying to retrieve an old suitcase from a heap of junk. My garage in Highbury. I know it's in there, Connie!

I woke and Carmen was beside me. She had brought

an armchair close. I realised at once that I was weaker and she stronger. Her eyes were steady, thoughtful.

Drink?

There was a glass of orange juice. I was shivering. She stood up, disappeared and returned with the bathrobe. She had ordered fresh sheets. I must sit in the armchair. She smiled a little mime. And I saw the room had been tidied. Everything was in order, chairs, tables, the things on the desk. Watching her change the sheets, I noticed a long black hair on the sleeve of the robe. Had she seen it? Had she seen the ring with its Arabic script, the hair-grip? And the roses. They were on the coffee table now in a green glass vase.

Okay, she said. She put something soft in my arms. I go in the bathroom. You . . .

It was a pair of pyjamas.

Returning, she slid an extra pillow under my head. My breathing was short, my heart beating fast. I sipped the juice. She watched me. Eventually I asked, You have news?

Not good.

She sat. I daydreamed. Where was Bibi? For a split second I had the idea Bibi had turned into Carmen. I almost burst out laughing. The cat would be on the balcony. Raising my eyes, I saw it was dark out there. Saturday had gone. This was the last night.

There was a strange singing in the stillness. Carmen was bent over her phone, messaging, her lips pursed, hair falling forward across her face. She pushed it back. It fell forward again. There was a ring on her left hand, I noticed. But which finger?

She waited, tapping a foot. The screen lit up. She read. She tugged at her hair. Then she was texting again. Very fast.

Your mother? My voice was hoarse.

I had surprised her. She looked up, an odd stare in her eyes. My mother is dead. When I was a girl.

It would be her husband then. It seemed extraordinary to me that I should be allowed to sit in such intimacy with this woman, to watch her so openly. While she wrote she frowned and her long throat tensed, then waiting for a reply she looked at me with a vague musing expression. But I had thought the same thought about Rachel. How is it such beauty is allowed to me?

Food came. She propped me up. I sipped the carrot soup.

She ate in the armchair, holding the tray on her lap, dabbing her mouth with a blue napkin. Bibi was at her feet. Then she watched while I finished: an old man in her father's pyjamas, hand trembling as he lifted the spoon to his lips.

We knew, she spoke carefully, this is possible.

I didn't understand.

This . . . risk.

The coma?

Yes.

And they won't let you visit. You can't see him at all?

She stood up. Can I? She picked up the cigarettes from the bedside table. Outside?

While she was gone, I realised I hadn't packed my bag. Could I ask her? I had brought so little it would hardly matter if I left everything behind. Hopefully I would have more energy in the morning. I could buy a phone at the airport. Take three aspirin before boarding. That should get the fever down.

When she came back she seemed more restless. The messages had stopped arriving. She wanted to talk perhaps, but had no words. There were things I would gladly have said. She made a phone call, speaking quietly and practically, plucking at her cardigan. Now she got up and moved around, still on the phone. I enjoyed the murmur of her voice. I had the impression it slowed my heartbeat. But she is talking about a dying man, I reflected. Nevertheless the words plashed and trickled like a gentle stream. I wondered if she loved the person she was talking to. If she realised how happy I was to listen.

She had turned out the main light. There was only the bedside lamp. Still talking softly, she propped herself against the desk for a while, then walked over to the window, so that I saw her shoulders, her face reflected in the glossy panes. Now she turned and moved again, skirt swaying. She seemed to be looking at the imitation Kirchner. At last she signed off the call, picked up the cat and sat with the creature on her lap, stroking it with both hands.

What is the name?

Bibi.

She spoke to the animal in Italian. Low liquid vowels. Bibi licked the back of her hand.

After a while, she said: That is my husband. At the telephone. She frowned. Ex-husband. He is a doctor.

I tried to respond but only sighed.

He is looking . . . she hesitated, at the . . . exams, scanning? . . . from the hospital.

And?

She shrugged. It is not good. We wait. Another exam. Monday.

I'm sorry, I said.

And you, Frank? Pain?

I took a deep breath. Big headache. And my chest. I pushed my hands between the buttons of the blue pyjamas.

She looked around the room. I stay here the night, okay?

Really? There is no need, I said.

It's okay.

Suddenly I felt alarmed. What time is it?

She looked at her phone. Nine and fifteen.

Tomorrow . . . I pulled myself up on an elbow.

Yes?

I have a flight. To London. Eight o'clock.

She sat up, concerned.

Evening? Morning?

Morning. I have a wake-up call, at five thirty. Linate airport.

She set the cat on the floor. Frank . . . You are ill.

I have to go home, I said. I can't stay here. I am alone. It's expensive. If I get worse, the hospitals are full.

But you are . . . *contagioso*.

I didn't know what to say.

At the airport they control the fever. She lifted a hand and pointed an imaginary gun.

We were really looking at each other now. She seemed shocked I would even think of going.

Perhaps it's not the virus. You know. Just flu.

You must make the test.

In London.

She fell silent and started to check something on the phone. Her fingers tapped. There was a fine intensity about her. Lamplight in her hair. She was searching for some important fact. Then she gave up. She came to the bed and put a hand on my forehead.

You are hot.

I'm okay.

She drew a deep breath.

I asked: Aren't you afraid of this illness, Carmen? I am very grateful, but you shouldn't stay the night here.

She didn't understand.

You are not scared? Not worried? Afraid. About the virus? The danger.

Oh. She pulled a face. I am . . . young. A woman. Good health. Tonight I cannot sleep. For my father. After that, *quarantena*. Then it occurred to her. Can you . . . ? She sniffed the air.

I hesitated. I'm not sure.

She turned and went to the desk, rummaged in her handbag. I heard the sound of a spray. Now the hand came close to my face again. Tracery of veins in a slim wrist. Blue bracelet.

I am sure it is lovely, I said.

Her eyes opened wide. Peperoncino spray!

Oh dear!

She laughed. Givenchy.

I sank back on the pillow and closed my eyes. Then after a moment, You know I thought Alberto was your husband.

I kept my eyes shut.

She smiled. Many people are thinking so. After a few moments she added: We are work partners many years.

Architects.

Yes.

Houses, offices?

We restructure, she said. In the old centre. We make old buildings new.

Work partners was an expression Rachel and I had used.

Neither of us spoke again. Shivering, I went to the bathroom. I propped myself against the wall over the loo. No question of cleaning teeth. I managed to gather toothbrush and things in my washbag. Stumbled back to bed.

Carmen had opened the wardrobe, found a blanket. The same I used last night. She was curled into the armchair. We settled for the night. And exactly as I closed my eyes I realised I had missed Deborah. She would have written an email, from the train. Perhaps phoned, from the station, a couple of hundred yards away.

On my back, I suddenly felt extremely lucid, close to some important truth. That evening with Deborah had been very fine. She was calling to me from a distance. I remembered the dinner table. Calling me back to society. It was flattering. Deborah is a good person, I thought. She and Dan worked as if civilisation depended on it. Someone was needed to replace him. In response, I had told her about Rachel, about the moment Rachel was gone. The moment in the morgue when you understand you will never speak to someone again. No, I hadn't told her that, but that was what I meant. And she had just seen Dan in his coffin. And so? And so?

I turned on my side and stared at the figure curled up on the armchair.

XXIII

Carmen picked up the phone. The wake-up call. I had spent the night in Shimla. Driving to Shimla. In the car the driver gave me a banana. I was hungry. Twelve hours later, at the door to the mortuary, a man handed me a business card: Deceased Repatriation, Safe & Speedy. And I decided instantly, in the teeth of her family's requests. No. Why? I have spent the night wondering why I made that choice. On the road to Shimla. The Indian dark sliding by. Men huddled by fires. A bus we could not overtake.

Grazie, Carmen said. She turned on the light. So?

I struggled onto my elbows and started to cough.

Frank. She stood at the end of the bed, skirt crumpled. Frank, *basta*. She made a performance of shaking her head, turning her face all the way to the left, all the way to the right. This . . . is . . . crazy, she said. A word for each movement of the head. *Stupido*. But still shaking her head she went to the wardrobe and pulled out my clothes.

Give me strength. I slid my legs over the edge of the bed and pulled myself up to a sitting position. She lay shirt and trousers on the quilt.

Stupido, she repeated, but began to push the other clothes into my bag. You are ill.

The pyjamas were soaking, the French windows shiny slabs of night. I got my shirt on but fumbled with the buttons. She came and did them up for me, half crouching.

You are crazy.

Now the cat was asking to go out. Carmen turned to the window while I fought to get my trousers on. Forget underwear. I fought nausea. I am going to do this. It was just a question of will. Some aspirin. Then I will be home. Where were my shoes?

The phone rang again and again she turned and picked up. It crossed my mind that she wasn't worried what people thought. Her being in Frank Marriot's room at this hour.

Grazie, she said. And to me: Taxi.

I found my watch. Five minutes early. But couldn't get to my feet. She went to the door, and came back with my stick. I put both hands on the pommel and was up. Shaky. We were face-to-face.

Frank. She bit her lip, exasperated. She doesn't look at all like Rachel, I thought.

You must not go.

I turned away to cough.

You are ill. Very.

The taxi is here now, I croaked. It was a strain to speak. And so?

From nowhere I remembered my passport. My passport expires next week. I must go now.

She shook her head. You want to die for a passport?

225

I leaned on the stick and shuffled towards the door.

Frank, I will stay with you. Here. Okay? Today, tomorrow. A week.

I had reached the door.

You are ill. I cannot see my father.

Now for the bag. Please, I asked. Could you? I'm stiff.

My father will die. And you?

I leaned on the wall.

Everybody is dying, she said. You don't know?

I thought about it. I looked around the room. It was 5.45. I put a hand on the handle. Go, not go. Either way was a step off a cliff.

Then my hand dropped. Okay, I said. It seemed I had decided. Okay, you are very kind.

She took my elbow, got me back to an armchair, then called Reception. As soon as I was sitting my head cleared. I felt better. I felt I could have made it. With a little effort. You said okay, I thought, because you want to be near this woman. You are taking advantage of her emotional distress. Surely it was crazier for her to stay near me than for me to take a taxi to the airport. Unless, I thought, it was her taking advantage of me, of my weakness. Was that it? She needed company. I needed a doctor. Which would be so much easier at home. Now my passport would expire.

I could change my mind perhaps. I drew a deep breath, but it seemed hard to get enough air. Like breathing through a thin straw. Carmen was still on the phone. How long can it take to cancel a taxi? I watched her. She was half sitting on the desk with her legs stretched out, bare feet, tousled hair. Mid forties, I thought. She listened, then spoke very clearly and sharply, giving instructions. Very professional. *Sì*, she repeated. *Sì, per favore.*

Breakfast arrived. Carmen brought the tray to the coffee table and shifted the armchairs either side. Croissants. Fruit salad. I nibbled.

I am getting better, I said. I remembered how quickly Omar had recovered.

She raised a hand, crossed her fingers.

Day was dawning now. She turned out the lamp and we watched the daylight come up.

Maybe some milk for the cat?

She didn't understand.

I took the saucer from under my cup, pointed at the milk jug. Bibi.

She smiled and provided. I watched her move. Then with eyebrows raised she asked, Why you have the cat? In the hotel.

I found it.

She made a face. And your hand? She pointed to the scratches on my wrist.

Too complicated. When I'm better.

Sitting back in my chair, I felt an immense sense of repose, after drama. The day felt kind. Carmen too appeared to lapse into some deep train of thought, eyes open, unseeing. So we sat together for some time. We make old buildings new, I remembered. At last she started to gather the cups and plates on the tray and asked, Why you come to Milan, Frank? Not the holiday.

I opened my eyes. A funeral.

Yes? She cocked her head.

An old friend. And work partner. A famous journalist. Magazine editor. From New York.

She seemed unconvinced. Milan? If he is New York.

He had a lover here. Buried here.

She didn't understand.

A woman, his lover, already dead, in the cemetery, here,
in Milan. He wanted to be beside her. Lie beside her. Dead.
Buried.

For a while she didn't speak. She looked at her
phone. Then said, For me, it is strange. My father will go
to the . . . *cimitero* at home. At Catania. With all the family.

He could still get better.

She stood up and took the tray to the door, put it
outside.

So the morning started gently. I was on the mend, I thought.
Carmen began her phone calls again, in an armchair or out
on the balcony, speaking quietly. For a while she left the
room. Perhaps to change her clothes. Half hour, she said.

Then the fever rose again. Again my chest grew tight.
I was thinking about what she had said, about being
buried at home. For the first time it struck me as quite extraordinary what Dan had done. Had there been some change
of heart, I wondered, at the end? Had he embraced my
pessimism? About his world. He often mentioned you,
Deborah said. A man who believed in his Round Table, I
thought, would let his knights bury him, surely, let them
cherish his remains and place him in their pantheon. You
left Rachel in Shimla, I realised, because we had both given
up on the world. Completely. At least on society. We were

so close to each other because so alien to the rest. Dan hadn't wanted anyone at his burial. That was the truth. Not me, not Connie. Certainly not Charles Porchester and the French philosopher. Perhaps not even Deborah. My breath was coming through sludge. The pillow was damp. I really don't care what they do with me, I realised. I just don't care.

Came a knock at the door. I thought so. Was it? Carmen had the key. Yes, a knock. I tried to lift myself onto an elbow. I was supposed to have checked out. I opened my mouth but could barely croak.

Now the journey darkened. There was marsh, heath, mountain. Now the slope was steeper. Ben thanked me for the money I had sent. A ridiculous spat with Connie. Sophie asked could I give her the balloon. The yellow balloon, Grandad! Then the boat was rocking fiercely. Water splashed.

You are awake? Carmen's voice.

Yes.

I was being washed. In bed.

How is it?

Okay. I'm okay.

I coughed. And coughed.

Eventually she said, A woman came.

Ah. Who?

I don't know.

She was sponging my back, my thighs. Cooling my body. Seeing all of me, I thought. Now there was the towel. At last she asked me to sit up. There were fresh pyjamas. For a moment we were face-to-face.

This woman said she . . . left? lost? . . . in the room, a ring.

Ah. You gave it to her.

Yes. On the desk.

Good.

Time passed. Only breathing mattered. I knew Carmen was in the room because I heard her voice. At one point I heard her crying. Then I wanted to tell her that I had got myself a stick because I had seen her father with a stick. I wanted to thank her, it had been so useful.

The television was on. I heard newsy noises. Alarms. But far away. I was underground, sucking in air through a crack.

Frank?

It was dark.

Frank, I call the ambulance. You are bad.

No. I'm okay.

You need the hospital.

I realised she was holding my hand.

I'm okay. I'm happy here.

It is two hours you are very bad. I will call now.

I tried to focus.

I am . . . afraid, Frank.

At last I found some breath. And a moment of clarity. So, here we are, I realised. Yes. Here we are. I recognised the place and gripped her hand.

Okay. Call.

She was speaking on the phone. Then she was beside me again. I felt her fingers, opened my eyes.

230

I have called.

Let's go. I'm ready.

I tried to get up.

Frank. Calm. They are busy. They come . . . later.

I lay still. Crushed by a great weight, but strangely cheerful. At some point I remembered: My stick, Carmen. Give back my stick to the lady in Reception.

Born in Manchester, **Tim Parks** grew up in London and studied at Cambridge and Harvard. He lives in Milan. He is the acclaimed author of novels, non-fiction and essays, including *Europa*, *A Season with Verona*, *Teach Us to Sit Still*, *Italian Ways* and *The Hero's Way: Walking with Garibaldi from Rome to Ravenna*. He has been shortlisted for the Booker Prize and has won many awards for both his work in English and his translations from the Italian, which include works by Alberto Moravia, Italo Calvino, Roberto Calasso, Antonio Tabucchi and Niccolò Machiavelli.